Joseph Ezekiel Rajpurkar

Kethoneth Yoseph

a hand-book of Hebrew abbreviations, with their explanations in Hebrew and English, for the use of students of the Oral Law and rabbinical literature

Joseph Ezekiel Rajpurkar

Kethoneth Yoseph
a hand-book of Hebrew abbreviations, with their explanations in Hebrew and English, for the use of students of the Oral Law and rabbinical literature

ISBN/EAN: 9783337316389

Printed in Europe, USA, Canada, Australia, Japan

Cover: Foto ©Andreas Hilbeck / pixelio.de

כתנת יוסף

שהיא

אסיפת ראשי תיבות

עם פרושיהם

בלשון הקודש ובלשון אנגליש

לתשוקת

התלמידים העוסקים בתורה שבעל פה

ודברי רבותינו ז״ל

מאת

הצעיר **יוסף יחזקאל** יצ״ו

מלמד בבית הספר של ה״ג **דוד ששון** נ״ע

סופר של חברת תקון בני ישראל

וחבר ליוניורסיטי של במבי

נדפס בעיר במבי י׳ע׳א׳

בשנת מה נמלצו לחכי ׳א׳מ׳ר׳תך מ׳ד׳בש לפי לפ״ק

בבית הדפוס של ה״ר יחזקאל בנימין פינכר הי״ו

KETHONETH YOSEPH.

A

HAND-BOOK

OF

HEBREW ABBREVIATIONS,

WITH THEIR EXPLANATIONS

IN

HEBREW AND ENGLISH,

FOR THE USE OF

STUDENTS OF THE ORAL LAW AND RABBINICAL LITERATURE.

BY

JOSEPH EZEKIEL,

HEAD MASTER, DAVID SASSOON BENEVOLENT INSTITUTION;

SECRETARY TO THE BENE-ISRAEL IMPROVEMENT

SOCIETY;

AND

FELLOW OF THE UNIVERSITY OF BOMBAY.

BOMBAY:

PRINTED AT THE

ANGLO-JEWISH AND VERNACULAR PRESS.

(Opposite Musjid Bunder Railway Station).

1887—5647.

Price 2 Rupees.

מנחה היא

אל

ראשי בית הספר

הנוסד על ידי

המרוחם הגביר דוד ששון נ"ע

אשר הם

אבירי הרועים אשר לדוד

המתנדבים ברצון טוב ובנפש חפצה למלאכת

הלמוד ולעניני צדקה וחסד

לתשואות חן

ולאות אהבה וכבוד

מאת

המחבר הצעיר יוסף יחזקאל יצ"ו

DEDICATED

TO THE

PATRONS

OF THE

DAVID SASSOON BENEVOLENT INSTITUTION,

WHO LIBERALLY PROMOTE THE CAUSE OF EDUCATION

AND

HUMANITY IN GENERAL,

AS A TOKEN OF

GRATITUDE, AFFECTION AND RESPECT,

BY

JOSEPH EZEKIEL,

THE AUTHOR.

PREFACE.

Of all literatures, the Hebrew is, I think, the most difficult to master. Its student has to surmount numerous obstacles before he can acquire any degree of freedom with the idiom and the phraseology of its language. Except the Holy Scripture and the Liturgy, almost all Hebrew works are printed in Rabbinical round characters, and these, too, without any vowel-points. It is well known that words of this kind can be read in several ways: consequently the student has with great difficulty to make out the true reading and sense of such words from the context. Again, the language in which most Hebrew works are written, though generally it goes under the common name of Hebrew, presents certain diversities of dialect and style.

But the greatest difficulty is the short and abbreviated forms of certain words and phrases, and the names of Rabbies, and their works; which, again, are not used by every writer in the same uniform way. As every author is at liberty to contract any words or phrases he likes, the student is often utterly at a loss. But a good writer who coins any new abbreviations, uses the original words and phrases first in their complete forms before using their contractions.

Such Abbreviations are generally marked by two oblique strokes over them; but as words used technically, rhetorically, and in other special ways, are also marked with similar strokes, it is often most difficult to distinguish between them. Some, however, take but one stroke and show thereby that they want only their terminations. The student has also to use his discretion as to where a servile letter may or may not be included.

It is only for the use of tyros in Hebrew literature, and purely with the object of removing this last and the greatest difficulty, which I myself had to experience for a long time, and not at all with the object of displaying my knowledge either of Hebrew or of English—the former of which being self-acquired is but limited, and the latter, not being my own tongue, is not one in which I can claim to be proficient—that I have ventured to give publication to this little HAND-BOOK OF HEBREW ABBREVIATIONS. I therefore hope that the learned will connive at the errors that (besides those given in the *errata*) may have crept into this my first attempt—which is also, I believe, the first attempt that has been made in this direction at all—to present this little work to the public. And I should most thankfully welcome the kindness of any of my readers who would send me corrections or suggestions which might tend to make a second edition more accurate and useful, should I receive enough encouragement, in the approval of my readers, and in the sufficient sale of the present issue, to warrant me in attempting a second one.

J. E.

Initials used in this work:—

N. B.=Name of a Book.
N. P.=Name of a Person.
N. Pl.=Name of a Place.
N. R.=Name of a Rabbi.

ראשי תיבות

HEBREW ABBREVIATIONS.

א Stands for 1; as a sign of the 1st person singular future; also for אחד one; אלף thousand; אייר air; אדם man; אמר he said.

א"א = אני אומר I say, אדני אבי my honoured father; אומר אליהו says Elijah; אמר אחד says one; אפן אחד a means, way or manner; אל אמת the true God; אי אפשר impossible; אמן אמן Amen Amen; אשת איש wife of a man; אי אמרת if you say; אי אמרינן if we say; אין אומרים they do not say; אברהם אבינו our father Abraham; אילת אהבים a lovely hind (a loving address to a woman); אבי אסף the father of Asaph; N. B; ארך אפים long suffering; ארך אנפין long face; smiling countenance; long suffering.

א"אא = אלא אי אמרת but if you say.

א"אב = אי אמרת בשלמא if you say or state at full length.

א"אזל = אדני אבי זכרונו לברכה my honoured father of blessed memory; (used by a son when speaking of his deceased father).

א"אכ = אלא אם כן unless thus or in this way.

א"אס = אמן אמן סלה Amen Amen Selah or for ever.

א"אע = אברהם אבן עזרה Abraham Eben Ezra.

אא"עה = אברהם אבינו עליו השלום our father Abraham, may peace be on him.

אא"שי = אדני אבי שיאריך ימים my honoured father, may he prolong his days or life.

א"ב = אלפא ביתא the alphabet ; אל ברוך the blessed God.

א"ב א"ב א"ב = אחד בתורה אחד בנביאים אחד בכתובים one (passage) in the Law, one in the Prophets, one in the Hagiographa.

א"בא = אי בעית אימא if you want me to say; אחור באחור back to back.

אבב"שיי = אתרוג בצים בשר שמן יין ישן citron, eggs, fat meat, old wine.

א"בד = אב בית דין the president of a tribunal.

א"בה = אמר ברוך הוא He (God) who is blessed says; אבן העזר the stone of help; N. B. one of the parts of שלחן ערוך

א"בו = אדם בשר ודם man is flesh and blood or mortal.

אב"יה = אליעזר בר יוסי הגלילי Eliezer the son of Yose the Galilean.

אב"יי = אשר בך ירחם יתום Thou (O God) in whom the fatherless findeth mercy; אתרוג בצים יין ישן citron, eggs, old wine.

אב"יע = אצילות בריאה יצירה עשיה emanation, creation, formation, action.

א"ג = אית גורסין some read; אין גורסין they do not read.

אג"לא = אתה גבור לעולם אדני Thou art mighty for ever O Lord.

א"גס = אית גרסת ספרים some books read thus; אגב סודר on a handkerchief (form of an oath).

א"גר = אית גסות רוח there are some of haughty spirit; אגרות רמבם Maimonides's letters; N. B.

א"גש = אית גזרה שוה there is an analogy; אגרות שמואל Samuel's letters; N. B.

א"ד = איכא דאמרי there are some who say; אי דלמא if perhaps.

א"דה = אגרות דופי הזמן letters about the slander or ruin of the time; N. B.

אד"הר = אדם הראשון the first man or Adam.

א"דז = אדרא זוטא the smaller meeting room; N.B.

א"דם = אדם דוד משיח Adam, David, Messiah; אפר דם מרה dust, blood, bile.

אד"מו = אדם מופלג a man of distinction; אדם מובהק a famous man.

אד"עה = אמר דוד עליו השלום says David, may peace be on him.

א"דר = אדרה רבא the larger meeting room; N. B.

א"ה = אמר הפסוק the sentence says; אפילו הכי though it be so; אי הכי if so; not so; אליהו הנביא Elijah the prophet; אומות העולם the nations of the earth; *i. e.* the gentiles; אמר הכותב the writer says אב הרחמים the merciful Father; אבן העזר the stone of help; N. B. one of the parts of שלחן ערוך

אה״בה = אמר הקדוש ברוך הוא says the holy and blessed One (God).

אה״וי = אהובי וידידי my friend and beloved; my dear friend.

א״וע = אהובי ויריד נפשי my friend and beloved of my soul.

א״הח = אור החיים the light of the living.

א״הנ = אהובי נאמן my faithful friend; אין הכי נמי yes, it is also so.

א״הק = ארץ הקדשה the Holy Land.

א״הר = אהבה רבה great love; the portion of prayer commencing with the words אהבה רבה

א״ו = אדם וחוה Adam and Eve; אסור והתר prohibition and permission.

א״וא = אלהינו ואלהי אבותינו our God and the God of our fathers; אבה ואמה father and mother; אמת ואמונה truth and certainty; אחד ואחד one by one.

א״וה = אור השם the light of God; N. B; אמות העולם people of the world *i. e.* the gentiles; אסור והתר הארוך the prohibitive and permissive (laws) enlarged.

א״וח = אורח חיים the way of life; N. B. one of the parts of שלחן ערוך

או״כיר = אמן ואמן כן יהי רצון Amen and Amen may such be (His) will.

א״וע = אור עיני the light of my eyes (a loving address from a father to his child).

א״ופ = אופן wheel, means, manner.

או״רת = אומר רבינו תם our Rabbi Tam says.

א״ות = אורים ותמים Urim and Thummim; also N.B.

א״ז = אור זרוע sown light N. B; אליהו זוטא the junior Elijah; N. B.

א״זי = אזני יהושע the ears of Joshua; N. B.

א״זל = אמרו זכרונם לברכה say they (Rabbies) whose memory is blessed.

אז״ש = אזן שמואל the year of Samuel; N. B.

א״ח = אחד חסיד a pious man; אורח חיים the way of life; N. B. one of the parts of שלחן ערוך; אורחות חיים the ways of life; N. B; אסרו חג the day after a festival; אחד חסר one defective or imperfect.

אח״בי = אחינו בני ישראל our brethren the children of Israel; אחינו בית ישראל our brethren the house of Israel.

אח״דשו = אחרי דרישת שלומך וטובתך after wishing your peace and welfare (a form of commencing a letter.)

אח״זל = אמרו חכמים זכרונם לברכה say the wise men of blessed memory.

א״חכ = אחד חלוף כתב a different version writes; אחר כך after this.

אח״כא = אחר כך אומר after this he says.

א״חמ = אנן החומי מטה we the undersigned.

א"חפ = אזן חוטם פה ear, nose or muzzle, mouth.

א"ט = אבנים טובות good stones; N. B.

אט"בח = a cabbalistic commutation of the letters of the alphabet.

א"י = איתא there is; ארץ ישראל the land of Israel; איוב Job; אור יקרות the light of the precious; N.B.

א"יא = איש ירא אלהים a man fearing God.

א"יג = אמר יהודה גדליה says Judah Gedaliah.

א"יה = אם ירצה השם if God please; אם יעזור השם if God help.

אי"הב = אם ירצה השם בעבודתו if God be pleased in his service or worship; אם יגזור השם בחיים if God destine it with life.

א"יי = אברהם יצחק יעקב Abraham, Isaac, Jacob.

א"יש = אדני יתברך שמו God whose name is blessed.

אי"שר = אמן יהא שמיה רבא Amen, may His great name &c.

א"ית וכ"רת = אתה יי תשמרהו וכצנה רצון תעטרהו Thou, O God, protect him, and compass him with favour as with a shield.

א"כ = אם כן if so; איומה כנדגלות terrible as furnished with banners; N. B.

א"כח = אם כל חי the mother of all living.

אכ"יר = אמן כן יהי רצון Amen, may such be His will or pleasure.

א״כמ = אין כאן מקומו his or its place is not here.

א״כע = אכולי עלמא the public; the whole world.

א״ל = אמר ליה or אמר לו said he to him; * אין לומר not to be said; אם לאו if not; ארזי לבנון the cedars of Lebanon; N. B.

אל״בם a cabbalistic commutation of the letters of the alphabet.

א״לכ = אם לא כן if not so.

א״מ = אבינו מלכנו our Father, our King; אני מכוין I intend; אוהב משפט lover of justice; אחד מלא one complete or perfect; אבא מארי my honoured father; ארץ מצרים the land of Egypt; אספקלריא מאירא the shinning mirror; אור מקיף the surrounding light.

א״מו = אמור say.

אמ״זל = אמרו זכרונם לברכה say they (Rabbies), whose memory is blessed.

א״מן = אל מלך נאמן God the faithful king; אמרי נועם pleasant sayings; N. B.

א״מר = אמר רבי says Rabbi—

א״מש = אש מים שמים fire, water, heaven; אמרי שפר elegant sayings; N. B.

א״מת = איוב משלי תהלים the books of Job, Proverbs, Psalms.

אמ״תי = אמי מורתי תאריך ימים my honoured mother, may she prolong her days or life.

---

* This and all such phrases can be changed into all the genders, numbers and persons of the personal pronouns.

א״נ אם נאמר or אי נמי if we say; אין נופלים they do not fall (on their faces in daily prayers). אוצר נחמד delightful treasure; N. B; אור נערב mixed light N. B.

א״נך = אוריתא נביאים כתובים the Law, the Prophets, the Hagiographa; אורות נצוצות כלים lights, sparks, vessels.

אנ״כי = אשת נעורים כי תמאס when he hates the wife of his youth.

אנ״סו = אמן נצח סלה ועד Amen for ever, ever and ever.

א״ס = אמן סלה Amen for ever; אין סוף Eternity; also one of the Sephiroth or attributes of God.

א״ספ = אתנח סוף פסוק Athnah *i. e.* rest, (a tonic accent correspondings to a colon), Soph Pasuk *i. e.* end of a sentence (a tonic accent placed at the end a sentence corresponding to a period).

א״ע = אבן עזרא * Eben Ezra; the son of Ezra generally meant for Abraham Eben Ezra; אור עולם the light of the world; N. B; אהבת עולם eternal love; N. B; אמר עולא says Olla; את עצמו himself.

אע״נע = for אמר עולא נוחו עדן says Olla, may his rest be in Eden.

אע״ג = for אף על גב although.

א״עפ = אף על פי although.

א״עפכ = אף על פי כן although it be so.

---

* אבן is the Arabic form of the Hebrew בן son.

א"פ = אפשר possible.

א"פה = אפילו הכי though it be so.

א"פי = אפילו though.

א"צ = אין צריך it is not required; ארץ צבי the glorious or beautiful land; אורחות צדיקים the ways of the righteous; N. B; אהבת ציון the love of Zion; N. B.

א"צל = אין צריך לומר it is not required to say.

א"ק = אמר קרא the scriptural passage says; אור קדמון the first or original light; ארם קדמון the first or original man.

אק"בו = אשר קדשנו במצותיו וצונו who has sanctified us with his commandments, and has commanded us.

א"ר = אמר רבי or אמר רב says Rabbi—; אליהו רבא the senior Elijah; N. B; אפי רברבי the countenance of great men; N. B; אשלי רברבי the plantations of great men; N. B; אמר רבא says Rabba.

אר"א = אמר רבי אלעזר says Rabbi Elazar.

א"ראר"ית"א = אחד ראש אחדתו ראש יהודו אחד תמורתו one principal of his unity, one beginning of his individuality, his vicissitude is one.

ארג"מן = אוריאל רפאל גבריאל מיכאל נוריאל Uriel, Rephael, Gabriel, Michael, Nuriel (names of angels).

א"רזל = אמרו רבותינו זכרונם לברכה say our Rabbies of blessed memory.

אר"יבל = אמר רבי יהושע בן לוי says Rabbi Joshua the son of Levi.

אר"ל = אמר ריש לקיש says Resh Lakish.

אר"מע = אש רוח מים עפר fire, air, water, earth (the four elements.)

אר"ש = אמר רבי שמעון says Rabbi Simeon.

ארש"בג = אמר רבן שמעון בן גמליאל says Rabbi Simeon the son of Gamliel.

א"ש = אלה שמות these are the names ; N.B., אבן שואבת a magnet ; אמרי שפר goodly words ; N.B ; אלהינו שבשמים our Father who is in heaven ; אל שדי Almighty God ; אמונת שמואל the faith of Samuel ;N.B.

אש"ט = אמר שם טוב says Shem Tobe.

אש"עה = אמר שלמה עליו השלום says Solomon, may peace be on him.

אש"ש = אמר שמואל שולם says Samuel Shulam.

א"ת = אם תאמר if you say ; אל תאמר say not ; אור תורה the light of the law ; N. B ; אל תקרי read not.

את"בש = a cabbalistic communtation of the letters of the alphabet.

א"תל = אם תאמר לי if you say to me ; אם תמצא לומר if you find (any reason) to say.

אות ב

ב" = stands for 2 ; as a prefix it signifies on, in, with through, for, against.

ב"א = בני אדם the children of Adam or human beings; בית אב a family circle; בן אשר the son of Asher; *

* Ben Asher was a principal of a college of the Masorites who differed from Ben Naphtali in reading the Hebrew text of the scripture chiefly in vowel points and tonic accents.

בר אוריין a learned scholar of the Law; בר אבהן the son or descendant of scholar of the law; בני אהרן the sons of Aaron; בית אלהים the house of God. בית ראשון the first temple of Jerusalem

ב״אג = בית אהרן גרשון the house of Aaron Gershon; N. B.

ב״אה = בית אהרן the house of Aaron; N. B; באר היטיב well explained, (a commentary on שלחן ערוך).

ב״אי = ברוך אתה יי blessed art thou O Lord; בארץ ישראל in the land of Israel.

באי״אמה = ברוך אתה יי אלהינו מלך העולם blessed art thou O Lord our God, King of the universe.

באי״שת = ברוך אתה יי שומע תפלה blessed art thou O Lord hearer of prayer.

בא״נד = באין נגרע דבר having nothing wanting.

ב״אש = באמונה שלמה with perfect honesty, with perfect faith.

ב״ב = בעלי בתים house owners; members of a congregation; במהרה בימינו speedily in our days, בבא בתרא the hinder gate, a tract in the Talmud; בני בית household; תרין תרין two by two; ביני ביני meanwhile; by and bye.

בבד״הב = בספר בדק הבית in the book called Bedek Habbaith (repairing the breeches of the house).

ב״בח = בספר בית חדש in the book called Baith Hadash (new house); בבעלי חיים in or among living creatures.

בבת = בלתי בעל תכלית the Being that has no limit; the Infinite Being.

ב"ג = בגמרא in the Gemara; בן גמליאל the son of Gamliel; בת גר or בן the son or daughter of a proselyte בת גיורת or בן the son or daughter of a proselytess; בת גילה or בן delightful son or daughter; בישול גוים (food) cooked by gentiles.

בג"ד = בגין דא in order that.

בג"ה = בגבורת השם by the power of God; בגזרת השם by the decree of God; בגין הכי on such account.

בג"י = בגימטריא by numerical value.

בג"כ = בגין כך on such account.

בג"ר = בשלשה רישין with three heads; with three letters called Resh.

ב"ד = בית דין a tribunal or court; בסעדא דשמיא by the support of God; בסייעתא דשמיא by the help of God; בית דוד the house or family of David; בעל דברים one who has a law suit; an eloquent speaker.

ב"דא = במה דברים אמורים this is only applicable; this is understood; to what is this applicable?

בד"אה = בית דין אמות העולם a tribunal of the heathens or a heathen court.

ב"דה = בדבור המתחיל in the commencing word or matter.

בד"הב = בדק הבית repairing the breeches of the house; N. B.

ב"דח = בינה דעת חכמה understanding, knowledge, wisdom.

ב״די = בית דין ישראל a tribunal of the Israelites or an Israelitish court.

בד״למב = במנא דכשר למקני ביה on an article fit to be sworn upon.

ב״ה = בדברי הימים in the Chronicles; בית המקדש the holy temple; בית הכנסת a synagogue; בעל הבית the master of a house or host; ברוך המקום blessed be the Omnipresent; ברוך הוא blessed be He; ביאור המלה explanation of the term or word; בשם יי in the name of God; ברוך השם blessed be God; בית המדרש a college; בית הלל the college of Hillel; באר הגולה the pit of captivity, i. e. the tyrany during the dispersion; description of the captivity; N. B; בדק הבית repairing the breeches of the house; N. B; ברכת התורה blessing for the gift of the Law; בין השמשות the time of evening twilight.

ב״הא = בית הלל אומרים the college of Hillel says.

ב״הב = בעל הבית the master of a house or host.

ב״הג = בעל הלכות גדולות the author of Halachoth Gedoloth or greater rules.

ב״הז = ברכת הזבח the blessing of the sacrifice; N. B.

ב״הט = בעל הטורים the author or owner of the rows of precious stones; N. B.

ב״הכ or ב״הכנ = בית הכנסת a synagogue.

ב״הל = בית הלוי the house or family of Levi.

ב״המ = בית המדרש a college.

בה"מז = ברכת המזון grace after meals.

בה"מק = בית המקדש the holy Temple of Jerusalem

בה"נו = בשם יי נעשה ונצליח in the name of God shall we work and prosper; בשם יי נתחיל ונגמור in the name of God shall we commence and finish.

ב"הע = בית העזיאלי the house or family of Uzziel; בהעלותך the portion of the law from the beginning of chapter VIII of the book of Numbers to the end of chapter XII; בני העיר the inhabitants of the city.

ב"הק = בנין הקל a light building; the light conjugation (in grammar); בית הקברות a grave yard.

בה"קר = בר הקדוש רבי Rabbi—the son of (Rabbi-Judah) the holy.

ב"הת = בעל התרומות the owner of the heave offerings; N. B.

ב"ו = בשר ודם flesh and blood; a human being, a mortal.

ב"ובק = בעגלא ובזמן קריב speedily and in a short time.

בו"צומ = ברכה ושלום צדקה ומשפט blessing and peace, righteousness and justice.

ב"ז = בן זכאי (Rabbi Johanan) the son of Jaccai; בנימין זאב Benjamin is a wolf; N. B; בעבור זה on account of this.

בז"הל = בזה הלשון in this language.

ב"ח = בן חורין or בני חורין free man or free men בקור חולים visiting the sick; בעלי חיים living creatures; בעל חוב

a debtor; בית חדש a new house; N. B; בן חביב a beloved son; בני חייא the sons of Chiya; N. B.

בח"המ = בחול המועד during the middle days of a feast.

ב"חח = בחובה חמורה under obligation involving risk; בחרם חמור under a serious excommunication.

ב"חי = בחינה examination.

בחי"ע = בחינת עולם an investigation into the (moral) world.

ב"י = בני ישראל the children of Israel; בית ישראל the house of Israel; בית יעקב the house of Jacob; בית יהודה the house of Judah; בית יוסף the house of Joseph; ברכת ישראל the blessing (given by Moses) to the Israelites as mentioned in Deut. I. 11; בינה understanding, one of the ten Sephiroth or attributes of God.

בי"ד = בית דוד the house or family of David.

בי"לאו = ברוך יי לעולם אמן ואמן blessed be God for ever Amen and Amen.

ב"ימ = בשם יש מפרשים in the name of some commentators.

ב"יע = בית יעקב the house of Jacob; N. B.

ב"כ = ברכת כהנים the blessing to be given by the priests to the Israelites (as mentioned in Num. VI. 24-27 בתי כנסיות synagogues; בשביל כן on such account; באי כח executors; authorized or rightful persons.

ב"כי = בכתיבת יד in handwriting; in manuscript.

בכ״ימ = ברוך כבוד יי ממקומו blessed be the glory of God from its place.

בכ״מ = בכסף מלא in full price; בכל מקום in every place; בכסף משנה by double money; in the book called Keseph Mishne.

בכ״מד = בכמה דוכתי in several places.

ב״ל = בן לוי the son of Levi; בן לב the son of Leb; בינה לעיתים knowledge of the times; N. B.

בל״א = בלשון אשכנז in German language; בלישנא אחרינא in another language.

בל״אא = בן לאדני אבי the son of my honoured father.

בל״אה = בלאו הכי excepting this.

ב״לב = ברוך לעולם בוראנו blessed be our Creator for ever.

ב״לה = בלשון הקודש in the holy language; in Hebrew.

ב״לנ = בלי נדר without a solemn promise; בלא נכוי without any discount or deduction.

בל״עז = בלשון עם זר in the language of a strange people; בלשון עירנו זה in the language of our this city.

ב״מ = בר מנן far be it from us; בבא מציעה the middle gate, a tract in the Talmud; ברית מנוחה the covenant of rest; N. B; בית מועד the house of an assembly; N. B; בכל מקום in every place; בר מצוה son of religion; a youth who at the age of thirteen years, should assume the obligation of religious duty.

ב״מא = במקום אחר in another place.

ב״מג = במספר גדול by greater calculation, counting units as tens hundreds &c.

במ״דלב = במנא דכשר למקני ביה on an article fit to be sworn upon.

ב״מח = באר מים חיים a well of living water ; N. B.

ב״ממ = בורא מיני מזונות the Creator of varieties of food ; ברית מטה משה the covenant of the rod of Moses ; N. B.

ב״מק = במספר קטן by smaller calculation, counting tens and hundreds as units.

ב״מר = במדבר רבא the allegorical exposition of the book of Numbers, which is a part of מדרש רבא

במ״רזל = במאמר רבותינו זכרונם לברכה in the sayings or writings of our Rabbies of blessed memory.

ב״מש = במלות שונות in different word ; במה שאמר in what he said.

ב״נ = בר נש a son of man, a human being ; בן נפתלי the son of Naphtali ; * בני נח the sons of Noah.

ב״נד = בנימוס דילן according to our rule or custom.

בנ״חש = בנדוי חרם שמתא by or in Niddui, Cherem, and Shematta (the three different sorts of excommunications.)

ב״ני = בני ישראל the childern of Israel.

---

* Ben Naphtali was a principal of a college of the Masorites, who differed from Ben Asher in reading the Hebrew text chiefly in vowel points and tonic accents.

בנ"לך = ברוך נותן ליעף כח blessed is He who gives strength to the weary.

בנ"צב = בנכסי צאן ברזל with or in property like sheep considered as iron, i. e. liable neither to increase nor to decrease.

ב"נר = בורא נפשות רבות the Creator of numberless souls, a grace after drinking water or eating any kind of fruit; &c.

ב"ס = בספר in a or the book; בסוד in the assembly; in the mystery; שני ספירות two Sephiroth or attributes of God.

ב"סד = בסעדא דשמיא by the support of God; בסיעתא דשמיא by the help of God; בסוף דבר at the end of the matter or saying.

בס"חט = בספר חיים טובים in the book of happy life.

ב"סט = בסימן טוב in or with an auspicious sign or omen.

בס"פי = בסבר פנים יפות with a delightful countenance.

בס"תה = בספר תורת האדם in the book called Torath Haadam (the law of man); בספר תורת הבית in the book called Torath Habbaith (the law of building houses).

ב"ע = בני עיר or בן the inhabitant or inhabitants of a city; בן עזרה the son of Ezra; בן עוזיאל the son of Uzziel; בריאת עולם the creation of the world; ברית עולם an everlasting covenant; בית עולם an everlasting habitation i. e. grave; בית עשק the house of contention N. B; באר עשק the well of contention; N. B; N. Pl; בני עמינו the children of our people.

ב"עד = ברוך עוזר דלים blessed is He who helps the poor.

ב"עה = האל or בעזרת השם by the help of God; בעל הנס worker of wonders.

בע"הב = בעל הבית the owner of a house; or the host; בעולם הבא in the future world.

בע"הו = בעזרת האל וישועתו by the help of God and His salvation.

בע"הז = בעולם הזה in this world; בענין הזה in this matter.

בע"הית = בעזרת האל יתברך by the help of the blessed God.

בע"המח = בעל המחבר the author.

בע"הע = בעל העטור the owner of the crown; the author of the book called Ha-ittur.

בע"הר = בעונותינו הרבים on account of our numerous sins.

בעו"בזק = בעגלא ובזמן קריב speedily and in a short time.

בע"ובי = בעיר ואם בישראל in the city and mother town of Israel.

בע"והר = בעונותינו הרבים on account of our numerous sins.

ב"עח = בעלי חיים living beings.

ב"עכ = בעל כרחו being compelled.

בע"שג = בערכאות של גוים in the tribunals or courts of the gentiles.

בע"שית = בעשרה ימי תשובה during the ten penitential days.

ב"עת = בעזר עליון תבנה may it be built by the help of the Most High.

ב"פ = בורא פרי the Creator of the fruit of—; בן פלוני the son of so and so; שני פעמים twice.

בפ"הג = בורא פרי הגפן the creator of the fruit of vine.

ב"פי = בן פורת יוסף Joseph is a fruitful bough (used in expressing prosperity).

ב"פע = בפני עצמו by himself.

ב"צ = בעזרת צור by the help of the Rock; בשרתי צדק I have preached righteousness; N. B.

ב"צא = בצלאל אשכנזי Besalel Ashkenazy.

ב"ק = בת:קול a divine oracle; בבא קמא the front gate; a tract in the Talmud.

בה"זא = בקונטרים אחרון in the last notes or treatise; in the latter writing.

בק"ור = בקול רם with a loud voice.

ב"ר = בר רבי or בן the son of Rabbi—; בראשית רבא the allegorical exposition of the book of Genesis; which is a part of מדרש רבא

בר"הי = ברשות היחיד private place; private jurisdiction.

בר"הל = ברכת הלבנה the blessing said at the sight of the new moon.

בר"המז = ברכת המזון grace after meals.

ב"ש = בית שני the Second Temple of Jerusalem; בית שמאי the college of Shammai; ברוך שאמר blessed be He who said &c, the portion of the prayer which commences with the words ברוך שאמר; שני שלישים two thirds; ברוך שמו blessed be His name; באר שבע the well of an oath; N. B; also N. Pl; בית שמואל the house or family of Samuel; N. B; ברכת שמואל the blessing of Samuel; N. B; בר ששת the son of Sheshath; N. B;

ב"שא = בית שמאי אומרים the college of Shammai says.

בש"אח = בשם אחרים in the name of Rabbi Meer; in the name of others.

בש"ד = בשבועה דשמיא by swearing in the name of God.

בש"דא = בשבועה דאוריתא by swearing upon the Law.

בש"דמא = בשבועה דמר אתרא by swearing before the Rabbi of the place.

בש"הט = בשולחן הטהור in the clear book called Shulhan Aruch.

ב"שח = בשבועה חמורה by a solemn oath.

בש"יא = בשם יש אומרים in the name of Rabbi Nathan; in the name of some who say.

בשכ"מלו = ברוך שם כבוד מלכותו לעולם ועד blessed be the name of the Glory of his Kingdom for ever and ever.

ב"שר = בשם רבי in the name of Rabbi.—

ב"ת = בעל תכלית a finite being; בעל תשובה a penitent person; בל תוסיפו you should not add.

בת"ואר = בעוצם תשוקה ואהבה רבה with strong affection and great love.

אות ג

ג" Stands for 3.

ג"א = גור אריה a lion's whelp; N. B.

ג"ג = גרים גרורים drawn over or attracted proselytes

ג"ד = גין דא on this account; גזר דין a decree of a court of justice.

גר"מ = גדולת מרדכי the grandeur of Mordecai; N. B.

ג"ה = גין הכי on such account; גיא הנם the valley of Hinnom; hell; גזרת השם a divine decree; גבורת השם the power of God; גיד הנשה the sinew which shrank; גופי הלכות the substance of rules; N. B; גדולי העיר the leading members of a city.

ג"ז = גם זה this also.

ג"ח = גמילות חסדים acts of beneficence; שלשה חדשים three months.

ג"ט = שלשה טפחים three hand breadths.

ג״י = גימטריא the numerical value of the letters of the alphabet; שלשה ימים three days; גט ישן an old bill of divorce.

ג״כ = גם כן also so; גם כאן also here.

ג״נת = גימטריא נוטריקון תמורה numerical value of the letters, notarica, commutation of letters.

ג״ס = שלשה ספירות three Sephiroth or attributes of God.

ג״ע = גן עדן the garden of Eden; גלוי עריות incest; שלשה עליונות the three higher ones; the three higher or upper (Sephiroth or attributes of God).

ג״פ = שלשה פעמים three times; שלשה פסיעות three steps.

ג״צ = גר צדק a proselyte of righteousness.

ג״ק = גבי קרקע the surface of the ground.

גק״ור = גזרות קשות ורעות severe and calamitous decrees.

ג״ר = שלשה ראשונות the first three; the first three (Sephiroth or attributes of God).

ג״ש = גרסת שמואל reading according to Samuel; גזרה שוה analogy. *

ג״שא = גל של אגוזים a heap of nuts.

ג״ת = שלשה תחתונות the three lower; the three lower (Sephiroth or attributes of God).

---

* This is the second of the thirteen rules laid down by Rabbi Ishmael for expounding the Law, and which contain a complete system of Scripture logic.

אות ד

ד״ = stands for 4; for a sign of the genitive case; for אשר *who, which* or *that*; דרך way or manner; דרוש discourse; דרש allegorical exposition; דף folio.

ד״א = ארבע אמות four cubits; דבר אמת a true word or thing; דבר אחר another word or thing; another explanation; דרך אחר another way; דא איהו this is it; דרך אמת the right way; דרך אמונה the way o truth; the way of faith; דרך ארץ politeness or a mannerly behaviour; דבר אחד one thing.

ד״אכ = דאם כן which if so.

ד״אל = דאם לומר which if said; דאין לומר there is no one who says; דאין לפרט which is not to be specified; דאין לפרש which requires no explanation.

דא״לה = דאי לאו הכי which if not so.

דא״לכ = דאם לא כן which if not so.

דא״לתה = דאם לא תימא הכי that if you do not say so.

ד״בה = דברי בית הלל the sayings of the college of Hillel.

ד״בט = דבק טוב a good attachment; N. B; דברי טובים the sayings of the good; N. B.

ד״בש = דבר שמואל the word of Samuel; N. B דברי בית שמאי the sayings of the college of Shammai.

ד״ד = דברי דוד sayings of David.

ד״דמ = דינה דבר מצרא the law about the claim of a neighbour.

ד״ה = דברי הימים the Chronicles; דברי הכל sayings of all (and disputed by none); דרך הקודש the holy way; N. B; דבור המתחיל the commencing word or matter; דברי המתחיל the words of the beginner.

ד״הא = דהא אמרינן which, behold, we have said this is what we have said.

ד״המ = דוד המלך King David.

דה״עה = דוד המלך עליו השלום King David, may peace be on him.

ד״הפ = דהכי פירש which he thus interpretes.

ד״ון = דכר ונוקבא male and female.

ד״וש = דורש ושואל one who enquires and asks.

ד״ז = דבר זה this word or thing; דברי זכרון the words of remembrance; N. B;

ד״ח = דרך חיים the way of life; N. B; דגש חזק a strong or double Dagesh.

ד״י = דברי יוסף the words of Joseph; N. B; ארבע יסודות the four elements.

ד״ל = די למבין enough to one who understands.

דל״מאע = דע לפני מי אתה עומד know before whom thou art standing.

דל״תה = דלא תימא הכי which is not or cannot be said so.

ד״מ = דרוש משה the discourse of Moses; N. B; דרש משה Moses explained; N. B; דרכי משה the ways of Moses; N. B; דרך משל for instance; figuratively. דרך מליצה rhetorically.

דמשא = דמשק אליהו Elijah of Damascus; N. B.

ד"נ = דברי ניחומים the words or sayings of consolation.

ד"נד = דנראה דברו that his word or saying appears or becomes clear.

ד"ס = ארבע ספירות four Sephiroth or attributes of God; דברי סופרים the sayings of the scribes.

ד"סד = דסלקא דעתא (a matter) which can be supposed.

ד"סל = דסבירא ליה which he thinks.

ד"ע = דברי עצמו his own words; **דעת עצמו** his own knowledge or opinion.

ד"פ = דו פרצופין two faces or bodies.

דצ"חמ = דומם צומח חי מדבר silent, sprouting, living, speaking, i. e. mineral, vegetable, animal, man.

ד"צך ע"דש בא"חב = דם blood, צפרדע frog, כנים lice, ערוב a mixture of noxious beasts and vermin, דבר murrain, שחין boils, ברד hail, ארבה locusts, חשך darkness, בכורות (slaying) the first born; the ten plagues brought upon the Egyptians.

ד"ק = דגש קל light or single Dagesh.

דק"יל = דקיימא לן which is confirmed with us.

ד"ר = דברי רבי the sayings of Rabbi—; דברי רבותינו the sayings of our Rabbies; דברי רבות matters of dispute; דברים רבא the allegorical exposition of the book of Deutronomy which is a part of מדרש רבא.

ד"רג = דרבינו גרשום according to our Rabbi Gershom.

ד"רו = דרוש discourse.

דרי"בב = דברי רבי יהודה בן בצלאל the sayings of Rabbi Judah the son of Besalel.

ד"ריל = דברי רבי יהודה לוי the words of Rabbi Judah Levi; דרשות רבי יהודה לוי the discourses of Rabbi Judah Levi.

ד"רמ = דרכי משה the ways of Moses; N. B.

ד"רנ = דרשות רבינו נסים the discourses of our Rabbi Nissim.

ד"רע = דברי רבי עקיבא the sayings of Rabbi Akiba.

ד"רש = דברי רבי שמואל the sayings of Rabbi Samuel; דרשות רבי שמואל the discourses of Rabbi Samuel.

ד"רשי = דרבי שלמה ירחי according to Rabbi Solomon Yarchi; דרבי שלמה יצחקי according to Rabbi Solomon Ishaki.

ד"רת = דרבינו תם according to our Rabbi Tam.

ד"ש = דברי שלום words of peace, דורש שלומך one who seeks your welfare; דבר שמואל the word of Samuel; N. B.

ד"שח = דברי שמעו חזון the commencing words of the three Haphtaroth of the three Sabbaths before the fast of the ninth of Ab.

דש"למ = דבר שיש לו מתירין a thing which is allowed by some in some instances.

דת = דברי תורה words of the Law; matters concerning the Law.

אות ה

ה״ = Stands for 5; as a sign of interrogation and as the definite article.

ה״ = יי or השם God.

ה״א = הוא אמינא we were saying; we would have said; הליכות אל the ways of God; N. B; הר אלהים the hill of God; N. B; האחד the one; הראשון the first.

הא״הל = המלה אשר הונחה להורות the word which is used to show.

האמ״וצ = האמת וצדק the true and just,

ה״אע = החכם אבן עזרא the wise Eben Ezra,

ה״ארי = הקדוש אלהי רבי יצחק לוריא the holy and godly Rabbi Isaac Luria.

ה״ב = הבא בעבירה he who commits a trespass or sin.

ה״בע = הכא במאי עסקינן what are we engaged with here; what do we speak about here,

הב״על = הבא עלינו לטובה that comes to us for good; הבא עלינו לשלום that comes to us for peace, or welfare.

ה״ג = הגביר the rich man; הלכות גדולות the great rules; N. B; הכי גרסינן thus we read; חמשה גבורות five powers.

ה"גא = הגהות אשירי a critical exposition of Rabbi Asher.

הג"ונ = הגביר ונעלה the rich and noble (gentleman).

הג"ינ = הגהות יש נוחלין a critical exposition of the eighth chapter of Gemara Baba Bathra which commences with the words יש נוחלין

ה"גמ = הגהות מיימוני a critical exposition of Maimonides; הגהות מרדכי a critical exposition of Mordecai.

הג"מנ = הגהות מנהגים a critical exposition of the customs.

ה"ד = היינו דכתיב this is the same what is written; הוא דאמרי it is he who said; הכי דמי it resembles thus; היכי דמי how does it resemble?

ה"דא = היינו דאמרי אנשי this is the same what those that speak in proverbs say.

ה"ה = הוא הדין this is the rule or judgment; היינו הך that is thus; האיש הגדול the great man; הלא הוא is it not he? הוא הדרך that is the way; הרב המגיד the Rabbi who informs; the editor of a newspaper; השר המרומם the exalted prince.

ה"הד = הדא הוא דכתיב this is what is written; as it is written; היינו הא דכתיב this is the same which is written; היינו הך דאיתמר this is the same what is said.

הה"כו = הרב הכולל the chief Rabbi.

ההמ"כ = האיש הגדול מנוחתו כבוד the great man, may his rest be glorious, a phrase used after the name of a deceased person.

ה"הק = היכל הקדוש the holy temple.

הה"קק = היכל הקדוש קבלה the holy temple, a tradition; N. B.

ה"הר = החכם הגדול רבי the great wise man Rabbi—;

ה"וד =.הוא דכתיב this is what is written.

ה"ול = הוה ליה he had.

הו"שר = הושענה רבה the great Hoshana or the seventh day of the feast of tabernacles.

ה"ז = השביעי the seventh; הרי זה behold this; behold this is considered; היינו זה that is this; הררת זקנים the glory of the aged; N. B.

ה"ח = חמשה חסדים five mercies.

הח"ו = החכם ושלם the wise and perfect or devout—

הח"ונ = החכם ונבון the wise and prudent.—

ה"ט = הלכות טוען the rules of arguing; also N. B.

ה"י = השם יתברך the blessed God; השם ישמרהו may God protect him; השם יתעלה may God be exalted.

ה"יו = השם ישמרהו ויחיהו or ויצילהו may God protect him and grant him long life or deliver him.

הי"ול = היוצא לאור which is published.

הכ"דא = היכמא דאמר this is just as he said.

הכ"הג = הכהן הגדול the high priest.

הכ"והצ = הכבודה והצנועה the honored and chaste (woman).

הכ"וח = הכותב וחותם he who writes and signs.

ה"כמ = הכתוב מטה that which is written below.

ה"ל = היה לו or הוה ליה he had.

הל"כת = המשתחוה לכבוד תפארתך he who bows down to the honour of thy glory.

הי"לל or ה"לל = היה לו לומר or הוה ליה למימר he had to say; he ought to have said.

ה"למ = הלכה למשה מסיני rule (given) to Moses on Sinai.

הל"מש = הוי ליה מחויב שבועה he was obliged to be sworn.

הל"קט = הלכות קטנות smaller rules.

ה"לש = הושיענו למען שמך save us for thy name's sake.

ה"מ = הואיל משה Moses was willing; N. B; המלכות the kingdom; המלה the word; הני מלי the words (are applicable to); הכי מאי what is this; הברה מורכבת a compound syllable; הפסד מרובה a great loss or damage; המרוחם one who has obtained mercy, a phrase used before the name of a deceased person.

המ"בה = המקום ברוך הוא the Omnipresent who is blessed.

המ"ול = המוציא לאור the publisher.

המ"ונ = המשכיל ונבון the intelligent and prudent.

ה"ממ = הרב מגיר משנה the deputy or delegate Chief Rabbi; the author of Maggid Mishne.

המ"עבד = המעשה בית דין the work of a tribunal.

המ"עה = המוציא מחברו עליו הראיה he who proves (his claim) by the evidence of his companion.

ה"נ = הכי נמי also so; **הלכות נדה** the laws concerning menstrual uncleanness.

הנ"בא = הנשבעים באמת those who swear in truth

הנ"וח = הנבון וחכם the prudent and wise; הנבון וחשוב the prudent and esteemed.

ה"נז = הנזכר the said.

הנ"זל = הנזכר לעיל or למעלה the abovementioned.

ה"נר = הנעלי רבי let my Rabbi enter.

ה"ס = חמשה ספירות five Sephiroth or attributes of God; הר סיני Mount Sinai.

הס"הפ = הסכמת הפוסקים the approval or sanction of the arbiters.

הס"רהפ = הסכמת רוב הפוסקים the approval or sanction of most of the arbiters.

ה"ע = הליכות עולם the ways of the world; N. B.

ה"עה = העולם הבא the future world.

הע"הז = העולם הזה this world.

ה"פ = הכי פירש it is thus interpreted or explained; הברה פשוטה a simple syllable.

ה"פמ = הפסד מרובה a great loss or damage.

ה"צ = הצעיר the humble or small.

ה"ק = הא קשה this is difficult, הכי קאמר thus he says; האי קרא this is the passage; הדרת קודש the Holy Majesty; N. B; הלכות קטנות the smaller rules; הכי קשה thus he objects.

הק"בה = הקדוש ברוך הוא the holy and blessed One.

הק"ל = הקודם לבא he who comes first.

הק"מל = הכא קא משמע לן here it appears to us; here it teaches us.

ה"קר = הקדוש רבי the holy Rabbi—.

ה"ר = הושענה רבה the great Hoshana or the seventh day of the feast of tabernacles; הרב רבי or רבינו my or our learned Rabbi, a phrase used before the name of a learned man; הקדמת רמבם the proposition, preface or introductory remarks of Maimonides.

הר"אבד = הרב רבי אברהם בן דוד the learned Rabbi Abraham the son of David.

הר"אה = הרב רבי אהרון הלוי the learned Rabbi Aaron the Levite.

הר"אבח = הרב רבי אליהו בן חיים the learned Rabbi Elijah the son of Haeem.

הר"אמ = הרב רבי אליהו מזרחי the learned Rabbi Elijah Mizrachi; הרב אספקלרייא מאירה the author of Aspaklarya Meira.

הר"אש = הרב רבינו אשר our learned Rabbi Asher.

הר"בי = הרב בית יוסף the author of Beth Yoseph.

הרד"בז = הרב רבי דוד בן זמרא the learned Rabbi David the son of Zimra.

הר"זה = הרב רבי זרחיה הלוי the learned Rabbi Zerachya the Levite.

הר"יפ = הרב רבי יצחק אלפסי the learned Rabb Isaac Alphasi.

הר"מבם = הרב רבי משה בר מיימון the learned Rabbi Moses the son of Maimon, commonly called Maimonides.

הר"מבן = הרב רבי משה בר נחמן the learned Rabbi Moses the son of Nachman, commonly called Nachmanides.

הר"מדל = הרב מנחם די לונזאנו the learned Rabbi Menahem de Lonzano.

הר"מה = הרב רבי מאיר הלוי the learned Rabbi Meir the Levite.

הר"מק = הרב רבי משה קורדובירו the learned Rabbi Moses Kordovero.

ה"רן = הרב רבינו נסים our learned Rabbi Nissim.

ה"רש = הרב רבינו שלמה our learned Rabbi Solomon.

הר"שב = הרב שלום בוזאגלו the learned Shalom Bozaglo.

הרש"בא = הרב רבי שלמה בן אדרת the learned Rabbi Solomon the son of Addereth.

ה"ש = הגדת שמואל the allegorical narration of Samuel.

ה"שי = השם יתברך the blessed God.

ה"ת = הולך תמים one who walks uprightly.

ה"תז = הקדמת תיקוני זהר the preface or introductory remarks on Tikkone Zohar.

אות ו

ו" stands for 6; at the commencement of a word for the conjunction and; and at the end as the suffix of the third person.

וא"חכ = ואחר כך and afterwards.

וא"ילו = ואינו יכול להשבע ומשלם and one who cannot be sworn must return (the thing he has robbed from his neighbour).

ואכ"מל = ואין כאן מקום להאריך and this is not the place to lengthen the matter.

ו"אל = ואין להקשות and it is not to be disputed or argued; ואין לומר and it is not to be said; ואמר ליה and he said to him; ואם לאו and if not.

וא"עי = ולאין אונים עצמה ירבה and to those who have no might He increaseth strength.

וא"צל = ואין צריך לומר and it is not required to be said.

ו"אש = ואלה שמות and these are the names; the name of the second book of Moses; i. e. Exodus.

וא"שר = ואלה שמות רבה the allegorical exposition of the book of Exodus; ואליו שלום רב and many compliments to him.

ו"את = ואם תאמר and if you say.

ובח"זו = ובספר חיים זכרנו וכתבנו or וחתמנו and remember and write or seal us in the book of life.

וב"תכ = ובתורה כתובה and written in the Law.

ו"גו = וגומר et cetra.

ו"ה = ווי העמודים the nails or hooks of the pillars; N. B.

וה"אר = והא אמר רבי and behold Rabbi—says.

והב"ריח = והפותח בלי רשות ידקרנו חרב and one who opens (this letter) without permission will be stabbed by a sword.

וה"ה = והוא הדין and that is the rule.

וה"יע = ויי יאיר עינינו and God will enlighten us (on the matter).

ו"הל = והוא ליה and it will be counted to him.

ו"המ = והני מלי and these words (are applicable to).

וה"מב = והואמובן בנקל and it is easily understood.

והמ"לביא = והמוליך לידו ברוך יהיה אמן and may he who carries (this letter) to the hand of the addressed person be blessed. Amen.

וה"מי = והמשכיל יבין and the prudent will understand; והמבין ידום and the intelligent will be silent.

וה"מל וה"בא = והמוליך לידו יברכהו השוכן בציון אמן and may He who dwells in Zion bless him, who carries (this letter) to the hand (of the addressed person). Amen.

וה"מל ת"עב = והמגיע לידו תבוא עליו ברכה and may blessing come upon him who delivers (this letter) in the hand (of the addressed person).

ו"הס = והוא סוד and it is a mystery.

וז"ל = וזה לשונו and this is his language; and these are his words.

וז"ס = וזהו סוד and this is the mystery.

וז"ש = וזהו שאמר and this is what he says; וזהו שכתב and this is what he writes; וזה שהזכיר and this is what he mentions; וזה שביאר and this is what he explains.

וחכ"א = וחכמים אומרים and wise men say.

וח"ל = וחרב לזרים and it is as a sword to others

וח"לב = וחרב לזרים בנדוי and it is as a sword of excommunication to others.

וי"א = ויש אומרים and some say.

וי"ח = ויש חולקים and some dispute; וידי חובתו and through his duty.

וי"ל = ויש לומר and it is to be said.

וי"מ = ויש מפרשים and some explain; ויכתוב משה and Moses wrote; ויחל משה and Moses besought; the section of the Law commencing from Exodus XXXII. 11. and read on fast days.

ויק"ר = ויקרא רבה the allegorical exposition of the book of Leviticus.

וי"ת = ויונתן תרגם and Jonathan translates.

וכ"ה = וכן הוא and thus he or it is.

וכ"הס = וכן הסכים and thus he approves or sanctions.

וכ"הפ = וכן הסכימו פוסקים and thus the arbiters approve or sanction.

ו״כו = וכולי and so forth.

וכ״כ = וכן כתב and thus he writes.

וכ״מ = וכן משמע and thus it teaches; and thus it appears; and thus it is understood; וכל מקום and every place; וכן מוכח and thus it is argued or refuted

וכמ״דאל = וכמאן דאמר ליה and according to him who said to him.

וכ״נ = וכן נראה and thus it appears.

וכ״נאה = וכנפש נאמן אהבתך and according to the wish of your faithful friend.

וכ״פ = וכן פסק and thus he decides.

וכת״חזל = וכתקון חכמים זכרונם לברכה and as ordained by wise men of blessed memory.

וכ״תי = וכןתרגם יונתן and thus translates Jonathan

ול״אעי = ולאין אונים עצמה ירבה and to them that have no might, He increaseth strength.

ול״בב = ולבני ביתי and to or of my household.

ול״ביא = והצנע לכת בית יי אלהיך and walk humbly to the house of the Lord your God.

ולכ״אבה = ואין להאריך כי אם בשלומך הטוב and there is nothing to add but about your welfare.

ולכ״אלש = ולכל אשר לו שלום and peace to every thing that is his.

ול״מד = ולמאן דאמר and to one who says.

ול״מה = ולא מן העשוי and (a tabernacle) made (long before) will not do for the purpose.

ול״מל = ולא מצי למימר and he will find (no reason) to say

ו"לנ = ולי נראה and to me it appears.

ול"עע = ולערוך ענין and to arrange the matter.

ול"פז = ולפי זה and according to this.

ומ"וצ = ומורה צדק and a righteous teacher.

ו"נב = ונעשה נבלה and it (i. e. meat) becomes a carcass (unlawful to be used).

וע"דא = ועל דא אסמוך and on this I rely.

וע"הס = ועמך הסליחה and you will excuse.

וע"יע = וחוסה על ישראל עמך and have compassion upon thy people Israel.

וע"ס = ועד סוף and to the end.

וע"פז = ועל פרוש זה and on this explanation.

ופ"גינ = ופורץ גדר ישכנו נחש * and a serpant shall bite him, who breaks an hedge, i. e. transgresses a rule.

ופפכ"ינ = ופתו פת כותיים יינו נסך and his bread is as the bread of the Cuthians, and his wine as offered to an idol (used of an excommunicated person).

ופ"ציח ול"תמ = ופי צדיקים יהגה חכמה ולשונם תדבר משפט and the mouth of the upright utters wisdom, and their tongue speaks justice.

ו"ק = ששה קצוות six extremities i. e. east, west, north, south, zenith and nadir; וקשה and stiff or difficult; and he objected

---

* Taking the word נחש as the abbreviation of נדוי הרם שמתא the different sorts of excommunications, one severer than the other, the phrase means, may he who breaks an hedge or transgresses a rule suffer these three excommunications.

וק"יל = וקיימא לן and it is confirmed with us.

ו"קל = וקל להבין and easy to be understood.

ו"רמ = וראש מתיבתא and the principal of a college; the president of a tribunal; ורב מופלג and a distinguished Rabbi.

וש"וש = ואתה שלום וביתך שלום peace be to thee, and peace be to thy house or family.

ו"שר = ושלום רב and much peace; and many compliments.

ושע"כזי = ושלום על כל זרע ישראל and peace be to all the seed of Israel.

אות ז

ז" Stands for 7.

ז"א = זרע אברהם the seed of Abraham; N. B; זכרון אהרון the memory of Aaron; N. B; זעיר אנפין small face; frowning countenance; זבחי אלהים the sacrifices of God; N. B.; זכרון אמת a true memory; N. B; זה אנו this is not it.

ז"אב = זכור את בוראך remember thy Creator.

ז"אז = זה אל זה one to another.

ז"ב = זמן במה what is the time; זה ברור this is clear or purified; זרע ברך the blessed seed.

ז"ג = זקף גדול the little elevator, a tonic accent corresponding to a semicolon.

ז"ד = זה דעת this is the knowledge or opinion of.

ז"ה = זהר brightness or splendour; N. B. *

* Zohar is a work on the secret Science of the Jews.

זה"אלי = זה השלחן אשר לפני יי this is the table which is before the Lord.

ז"הל = זה הלשון this (is the) language ; these(are the) words.

זהל"ציב = זה השער ליי צדיקים יבואו בו this is the gate of the Lord, into which the righteous shall enter.

ז"הק = זהר הקדוש the holy Zohar ; N. B. ;

ז"ון = זעיר ונוקבין the smaller and the female attributes.

ז"ז = זר זהב golden wreathe ; N. B.

ז"ח = זהר חדש The new Zohar ; N. B ; זהרי חמה the radiance of the sun ; N. B.

זח"ה = זאת חקת הפסח this is the ordinance of the Passover ; N. B.

זט"ה = שבעה טובי העיר seven best or leading members of the city.

ז"י = זרע ישראל the seed of Israel; זריעת יצחק the plantation of Isaac ; N. B.

זי"עא = זכותו יגן עלינו אמן may his merit protect us, Amen.*

ז"כ = זוקף כפופים He who raises those who are bent down.

ז"ל = זכרונם לברכה or זכרונו of blessed memory;† זה לשונו this is his language; these are his words ; זכור לטוב remembered for good.†

* This is a eulogy used after the name of a learned and pious deceased man.
† This is a eulogy used after the name of Prophet Elijah.

זלה"ה = זכרונו לחיי העולם הבא may his memory be for the future world.*

ז"לז = זה לזה one to another.

ז"מ = זרע מלוכה the royal seed.

ז"מז = זה מזה one from another; one than the other.

ז"ס = זה סדר this is the order or arrangement; זהו סוד this is a mystery; שבעה ספרות seven Sephiroth or attributes.

ז"עמ = זנות עבודה (זרה) ממון adultery, idolatry, riches.

ז"פ = זבח פסח the offering of Passover; N. B. זמן פרעון time of repayment.

זצו"קל = זכר צדיק וקדוש לברכה may the memory of the just and holy man be blessed.*

זצ"ל = זכר צדיק לברכה may the. memory of the just man be blessed.*

ז"ק = זרע קודש or זרעא קדישא holy seed; זרע קיים a permanent seed. i. e. children living to their full age; זקף קטן a tonic accent corresponding to a comma.

זק"א = זקן אהרון the beard of Aaron; N. B.

ז"ר = זית רענן a blooming olive,a phrase to express prosperity.

ז"ש = זהב שיבה the gold of Sheba; N. B; זבחי שלמים peace offerings; N. B.

---

* This is a eulogy used after the name of a learned and pious deceased man.

ז"שה = זה שאמר הכתוב this is what the passage or writing says; זה שאמר הפסוק this is what the verse says.

ז"ת = זה תוקפו this is his might; שבעה תחתונות the seven lower (attributes).

אות ח

ח" = stands for 8; also for חסר defective; חלק part or volume; חדושי novelties of–.

ח"א = חכמים אומרים wise men say; חלק ראשון first part or volume; חכמי אמת theologians or wise men well versed in Kabbala; חסד אברהם the piety of Abraham; N.B; חדושי אגדות new allegorical expositions.

חא"ה = חלק אבן העזר the part of שלחן ערוך called אבן העזר; חכמי אמות העולם the wise among the gentiles.

חא"ח = חלק אורח חיים the part of שלחן ערוך called אורח חיים.

חא"ת = חבור אור תורה composition of the light of the Law; N. B.

ח"ב = חרבן בית the destruction of the temple; חכמה בינה wisdom, understanding; חנוכת בית the dedication of a house.

חב"גג = חכמה בינה גדולה גבורה wisdom, understanding, greatness, power.

ח"בד = חכמה בינה דעת wisdom, understanding knowledge.

ח"בה = חבצלת השרון the rose of Sharon; N. B.

ח"בי = חינוך בית יהודה the dedication or initiation of the house of Judah; N. B.

חב"תמ = חכמה בינה תפארת מלכות wisdom, understanding, beauty, kingdom.

ח"ג = חסד גבורה grace, power.

ח"גת = חסד גבורה תפארת grace, power, beauty.

חג"תמ = חסד גבורה תפארת מלכות grace, power, beauty, kingdom.

ח"ה = חדוש העולם wonder of the world; חלול השם profanation of the name of God; חלוץ הנעל he that has his shoe loosed *; חכם הרזים a wise man acquainted with the mysteries of the Kabbala; חוט השני a scarlet thread; N. B; חובת הלבבות the duties of the hearts; N. B.

ח"המ = חול המועד the middle days of a feast; חשן המשפט the breast plate of judgment; N. B; a part of שלחן ערוך

חה"מפ = חול המועד פסח the middle days of the feast of Passover.

ח"ו = חס והלילה or חס וחלילה far be it; הס ושלום God forbid.

ח"וב = חכמה ובינה wisdom and understanding.

ח"וג = חסד וגבורה grace and power.

חו"המ = חול המועד the middle days of a feast.

ח"וח = חן וחסד favour and grace.

---

* See Deut. XXV. 5—10

ח״וי = חוות יאיר Chawwoth Yair; N. B; also N.Pl.

ח״ור = חכמי ורבני the wise men and Rabbies of—

ח״זל = חכמים זכרונם לברכה wise men of blessed memory.

ח״ח = חובה המורה obligation or debt involving risk.

ח״חמ = חלק חשן משפט the part of שלחן ערוך called חשן משפט.

ח״ט = חן טוב good favour.

ח״י = התימת יד the signature or seal of—; חיצונים outward things.

ח״יד = חלק יורה דעה the part of שלחן ערוך called יורה דעה

חי״דא = חיים דוד אזולאי Haccm David Azulai.

ח״יט = חדושי יוסף טראני new work of Joseph Tarance; notes by Joseph Taranee.

ח״יע = חק יעקב the statute of Jacob; N. B.

ח״כא = הכמים אומרים wise men say.

חכ״ש = חכמת שלמה wisdom of Solomon; N. B.

ח״ל = חוצה לארץ out of the (Holy) Land; all countries except the Holy Land; חזון למועד vision of the appointed time

ח״לב = הרם לזרים בנדוי excommunication by נדוי to others (who open the letter).

ח״ל בנ״חש ד״רג מה = חרם לזרים בנדוי הרם שמתא דרבינו גרשום מאור הגולה excommunication by Niddui, Cherem (and) Shemmatta, of our Rabbi

Gershom, the light of the captivity, to; others (who open the letter).

חלע"הב or ח"לה = חלק לעולם הבא a portion in the future world.

ח"מ = חתומי מטה or חתום the undersigned; חלקת מחוקק a portion of the lawgiver; N. B; חמד המש Moses desired or was delighted; N. B; חוקי משפט the statutes of judgment; N. B.

ח"מה = חוץ מן הנכרי except the stranger.

ח"מז = חוץ מזה except this.

ח"מי = חיים מאת יי life from God.

ח"מכ = חוץ מכבוך except your honour.

ח"נ = חצי נזק half damage.

ח"נה = חלה נדה הדלקה separating the first cake of the dough, monthly uncleanness, lighting the Sabbath lamp, the duties requiring particular attention of Jewish females.

ח"נכל ש"צם = חמה the sun, נוגה Venus, כוכב Mercury, לבנה the moon, שבתי Saturn, צדק Jupiter, מאדים Mars.

ח"ס = חטף סגול a vowel point called short or composite Segol.

ח"סל = חסד לאברהם mercy towards Abraham; N.B.

ח"פ = חטף פתח a vowel point called short or composite Patha; חותם פה one who signs here.

ח"פי = חסרי פא יוד defective verbs having the letter י for their first radical.

ח"פנ = חסרי פא נון defective verbs having the letter נ for their first radical.

ח"צ = חכם צבי Hakham Sevi.

ח"ק = חזות קשה a difficult vision; חטף קמץ a vowel point called short or composite Kamets; חברה קדישא a holy society; חצי קדיש half of the praise in the liturgy called קדיש

ח"קה = חקת הפסח the ordinance of the Passover; N. B; הנוכה קודם הבדלה (at the close of the Sabbath) the ·lamps of the Feast of Dedication should be lighted before saying the blessing for making distinction between the Sabbath and the week days.

ח"קצ = חסרי קצוות verbs doubly defective or verbs having the signs of defective verbs both at the beginning and at the end.

חר"נג = חדושי רבינו נסים גיטין new work of our Rabbi Nissim on the tract of the Talmud on divorce.

חר"שבא = חדושי רבי שמעון בן אברהם new work of Rabbi Simeon the son of Abraham.

ח"ש = חשק שלמה the desire of Solomon; N. B; חכמת שלמה the wisdom of Solomon; N. B; חלק שני the second volume.

ח"שו = חרש שוטה וקטון deaf, mad and young (are exempt from certain punishments).

חש"מל = חנפים שקרנים מספרי לשון הרע flatterers liars, slanderers.

אות ט

ט = stands for 9.

ט"א = טעם אחר another reason or object; טעות אחד one error; טל אורות dew on herbs; N. B.

ט"אח = טור אורח חיים a series of notes on אורח חיים; N. B.

ט"ב = תשעה באב the ninth day of the month of Ab or the Day of Lamentation.

ט"דט = טמירא דטמירין mystery of mysteries or the greatest mystery.

ט"ה = טובי העיר the best or leading members of the city.

ט"המ = טעמי המצות reasons or objects of the precepts; N. B.

ט"ור = טוב ורע good and evil.

ט"ות = טבי ותקולי pure and exact in weight (used of money).

ט"ז = טורי זהב rows of gold; N. B.

ט"חמ = טור חשן משפט a series of notes on חשן משפט; N. B.

ט"מ = טעמי מצות reasons or objects of precepts; N. B.

ט"מר = טעמי מצות ריקאנאטי reasons or objects of precepts by Reckanati.

טנ"תא = טעמים נקודות תגין אותיות tonic accents, vowel points, crowns,* letters.

---

* The flourishes on the seven letters שעטנז גץ are called תגין or crowns.

ט״ס = טעות סופר a clerical error; טעמי סוכות reasons or objects of the Feast of Tabernacles; N.B; תשעה ספירות nine Sephiroth or attributes.

ט״ק = טבעת קדושין the wedding ring.

ט״ש = טוען שקר an imposter; a pretender.

ט״שת ס״אב מ״עק ג״דד = טלה Aries, the Ram; שור Taurus, the Bull; תאומים Gemini, the Twins; סרטן Cancer, the Crab; אריה Leo, the Lion; בתולה Virgo, the Virgin; מאזנים Libra, the Balance; עקרב Scorpio, the Scorpion; קשת Sagittarius, the Archer; גדי Capricornus, the Goat; דלי Aquarius, the Water-bearer; דגים Pisces, the Fishes.

אות י

י״ = stands for 10; at the beginning of words a sign of the third person future; and at the end as a sign of the first person singular.

י״א = יש אומרים some say; they say; יונת אלם a dumb dove; N. B; יד אבשלום the Pillar of Abshalom; N. B; יראת אלהים the fear of God; ירא אלהים one who fears God.

יא״וא = יי אלהינו ואלהי אבותינו the Lord our God, and the God of our fathers; יהי אור ויהי אור let there be light, and there was light.

יא״יא = יי אלהינו יי אחד the Lord our God is one Lord.

יא"צ = יאהר צייט the anniversary of the death of a parent.*

י"ב = יודעי בינה men of understanding.

יב"בא = יבנה במהרה בימינו אמן may it be built speedily in our days. Amen.

י"בנ = יהושע בן נון Joshua the son of Nun.

יב"נה = יין בשמים נר הבדלה wine, perfume, lamp, and the distinction of the Sabbath from the common days.†

יב"ע = יונתן בן עוזיאל Jonathan the son of Uzziel.

יב"על = יבא עלינו לשלום may it come on us for peace or happiness.

יב"צ = יפרח בימיו צדיק may the just flourish in his days; יכון בצדק may it (the city or community) be established in righteousness.

יב"ק = יעננו ביום קראנו may He answer us on the day we call upon him; יחוד ברכה קדושה unity, blessing, holiness.

יב"ש = יבין שמועה he will understand the report; N. B.

י"ג = יש גורסין some read.

י"ד = יורה דעה it will teach knowledge; a part of שלחן ערוך

י"דנ = יהי דן נחש Dan shall be a serpent.

---

* A German idiom.

† These blessings must be said by every Israelite at the close of the Sabbath.

י"ה = יד המלך the hand or power of the king; N. B; יום הכפורים the Day of Atonement.

יה"בי = יקותיאל הכהן בר יהודה Yekuthiel the priest, son of Judah.

יה"ל = יהפכהו יי לטובה or לשמחה may God change it (i.e. the Day of Lamentation) into happiness or joy.

יה"ר = יהי רצון may such be His pleasure.

יו"הכ = יום הכפורים the Day of Atonement.

יוי"לא = יתברך ויתעלה לעולם אמן may He be blessed and exalted for ever. Amen.

יו"מ = יואל משה Moses is willing; N. B.

י"ז = יתעלה זכרו may His memory be exalted.

יז"ייא = יראה זרע יאריך ימיו אמן may he see his seed, (and) may he prolong his days. Amen.

י"ח = ידי חובתו through his duty; יום חול a common day; יש חולקים some dispute; ילקוט חדש a new purse; N. B; שמנה עשרה eighteen (blessings) i.e. the prayer offered in a low voice on common days.*

יח"ב = יעשה חכמה בינה he will work wisdom and understanding; he will act with wisdom and understanding.

י"ט = יום טוב a solemn feast day.

---

* This prayer originally consisted of eighteen blessings, hence its name. The nineteenth, which stands twelveth in order, was added by Rabban Gamliel of the first century; or as others hold by Rabbi Samuel the little, one of Gamliel's desciples as a deprication against slanderers and apostates. It is properly called תפלה prayer, and sometimes עמידה as it is offered in a standing position.

י"מצ = יום טוב צהלון Yom Tob Sahlon; N. P.

י"י = יד יהודה the hand or power of Judah; N. B; יד יוסף the hand or power of Joseph; N. B.

יי"ב וב = יאריך ימיך בטוב ושנותיך בנעמים may He prolong your days in happiness and your years in pleasure.

יי"יי = יגל יעקב ישמח ישראל Jacob shall rejoice, Israel shall be glad.

יי"לו = יי ימלוך לעולם ועד the Lord shall reign for ever and ever.

יי"נ = יין נסך wine offered to an idol.

י"כ = יפוי כח to make good one's title or authority.

יכ"בצ = יכון בצדק may it (the city or community) be established in righteousness.

י"ל = יש לומר it is to be said; יש להקשות some object; it is to be objected to.

י"מ = יש מפרשים some explain; יש מאמרות there are some passages; יציאת מצרים Exodus from Egypt; יחוד מלכות unity of kingdom; יסוד מלכות the basis of the kingdom; (the attributes) basis and kingdom; ידי משה the hands of Moses; N. B; יבוא מנחם the Comforter shall come; יפה מראה well favoured; fair looking.

ימב"ומנ = יהי מקורך ברוך ושמח מאשת נעוריך may thy fountain be blessed, and rejoice with the wife of thy youth.

ימ"ה = יוצא מן הכלל an exception to a general rule;

one who separates himself from the general body of the congregation.

ימ"חב"פמ = יפוצו מעינותיך חוצה ברחובות פלגי מים may thy fountains be dispersed abroad; and rivers of water in the street.

י"מת = יום מתן תורה the Day of the Gift of the Law; ימי תשובה the penitential days.

י"נ = יחיה נצח may he live for ever; יש נוחלין there are some who possess; the chapter of the Talmud which commences with the words יש נוחלין; יש נוהגים some have the custom.

י"ס = עשר ספירות the ten Sephiroth or attributes; יש סופרים some write; יש ספרים there are some books.

יס"ש = יסוד שירים the principle rules of poetry.

י"ע = יפי עינים having beautiful eyes or countenance.

י"עא = יעזרה אלהים may God help it; יכונן עירו or עירם אמן may He establish his or their city. Amen יכוננה עליון אמן may the Most High establish it, Amen ישמרה עליון אמן may the Most High protect it, Amen; יעמד עד אליה may it stand until the coming of Elijah;* ישמעלים עובדי אלילים Ishmaelites (and the) worshippers of images.

י"עד = יי עוזר דלים God is the supporter of the feeble or needy.

יע"וש = יעוין שם he may see or refer there.

יע"קב = יוצריך עושיך קוניך בוראיך thy Former

* These abbreviations are used after the name of a city.

thy Maker, thy Possessor, thy Creator.

יפ"כ = יפוי כח to make good one's title or authority.

יפ"ע = יפה ענף a fair branch; N. B.

יצ"הט = יצר הטוב good imagination.

יצ"הר = יצר הרע evil imagination.

י"צו = ישמרהו צורו וגואלו may his Rock and Redeemer protect him; ישמרהו צורו ויחייהו may his Rock protect him and grant him (long) life; ינצור צאתו ובואו may He watch his going out and coming in; יי צורי וגואלי God is my Rock and Redeemer; ישראל צדיק וישר Israel is just and upright.

יצ"י = יצירה formation.

יצ"ע = יי צבאות עמנו the Lord of Hosts is with us.

יק"ז = יין קדוש זמן wine, sanctification of the holiday, and the enjoyment of the season.*

יקנ"הז = יין קדוש נר הבדלה זמן wine, sanctification of the holiday, lamp, the distinction between the Sabbath and the common days, the enjoyment of the season.†

י"ר = יהי רצון may it be His pleasure; ילקות ראובני the purse of Reuben; N. B.

י"רה = ירום הודו or הודה may his or her glory be exalted‡ ירחם השם may God have mercy.

---

* These blessings are to be said by every Israelite on the evening of a holiday. The blessing for the enjoyment of the season is. שהחיינו

† These blessings are to be said by every Israelite on the evening of a holiday that falls at the close of the Sabbath.

‡ A eulogy added after the name of a ruling sovereign, prince or princess.

י״רמ = יהי רצון מלפניך may it be pleasing or acceptable to Thee.

יר״וש = ירושלים Jerusalem

י״ש = ירא שמים one who fears God; יראת שמים the fear of God; יין שרף intoxicating spirit; ילקוט שמעוני the purse of Simeon; N. B; ימח שמו may his name be blotted out.

יש״א = ישע אלהים the salvation of God; N. B.

י״שב ו״שמר = ישכון בטח ושאנן מפחד רעה he shall dwell safely, and shall be quiet from fear of evil.

י״שו = ימח שמו וזכרו may his name and his memory be blotted out.

י״שי = ישרש יעקב Jacob shall sprout; N. B.

י״של = יהי שמו לעד may his name live or last for ever.

י״שמ = ישמח משה Moses will rejoice; N. B.

י״שק = יום שבת קודש the holy Sabbath day.

י״שש = ים של שלמה Solomon's molten sea; N. B;

י״ת = יתברך blessed; יונתן תרגם Jonathan translates; יסוד תשובה the basis of repentance; יפה תואר a goodly person; ימי תשובה the penitential days.

ית״וית = יתברך ויתעלה may He be blessed and extolled.

ית״קק = ישעיה תרי עשר קינות קהלת Isaiah, the twelve minor prophets, Lamentations, Ecclesiastes. *

י״תש = יתברך שמו may His name be blessed.

* This abbreviation shows the books on finishing the reading of which the Israelites repeat the verse before the last, as they do not end with propitious passages.

אות כ

כ" = stands for 20; at the beginning of words, according to, as; and at the end, as a sign of the second person singular; also for כתב he wrote; writing; כתיב written.

כ"א = כי אם for if; but; כל אחד each one; every one; כה אמר thus says.

כ"או = כל אחד ואחד each and every one.

כא"לש = כל אשר לו שלום peace be to all that is his.

כא"רזל = כה אמרו רבותינו זכרונם לברכה thus say our Rabbies of blessed memory.

כ"ב = כל בו all in it; N. B.

כ"ג = כהן גדול a high priest.

כ"ד = כמה דאמר as he says; כמא דאתאמר as it is said; כל דבר every thing; כה דברי such are the words of; כדבור דמי it resembles the saying or word.

כ"דא = כמא דאתאמר as it is said.

כד"ארזל = כמה דאמרו רבותינו זכרונם לברכה as our Rabbies of blessed memory say.

כ"ה = כן הוא so it is; כהן הדיוט a common priest; כי היך for so; for even as; כסה הכבוד the throne of glory; כבוד הבריות respect of living creatures; כר הקמח a measure of flour; N. B.

כ"הא = כן הוא אמר thus he says.

כ"הג = כהן גדול a high priest; כהאי גוונא of this colour or kind; in this manner.

כה"למ = כהלכה למשה מסני according to the rule given to Moses on Sinai.

כ"הק = כתבי הקודש the Sacred Writings; the Holy Scripture.

כ"הר = כבוד הגביר רבי the honourable gentleman Rabbi—.

כה"רר = כבודהדב רבי the honourable and learned Rabbi—.

כה"תיה = כל הנשמה תהלל יה הללויה let every thing that has breath praise the Lord; praise ye the Lord.

כ"ו = כפתור ופרח knop and flower; N. B.

כו"חט = כתיבה והתימה טובה a good writing or entry and seal.

כ"וכ = כך וכך so and so.

כ"ומ = כוכבים ומזלות stars and planets or the signs of the Zodiac.

כ"וע = כלל ועיקר a general and first principle; at all.

כ"ז = כל זה all this; כל זמן all the time.

כ"ח = כלי חמדה costly vessels or articles; N. B.

כ"חב = כתר חכמה בינה crown; wisdom, understanding.

כ"י = כלי יקר a percious vessel or article; N. B. כל ימיו all his days; כנסת ישראל the congregation of

Israel or the Jwish church; כתיבת יד a manuscript; hand writing; כנפי יונה the wings of a dove; N. B.

כ"יר = כן יהי רצון may such be His pleasure.

כ"יש = כוס ישועות a cup of salvation; N. B.

כ"כ = כל כך so much; כן כתיב thus it is written; כן כתב thus he writes; כל כתב the whole writing כל כדנן all like this; כתר כהונה the priestly mitre.

כ"כע = ככולי עלמא as the whole world.

כ"ל = כלומר as to say; כל לשנא every language; whole saying.

כ"לח = כי לעולם חסדו for His mercy endureth for ever.

כ"לי = כהן לוי ישראל a Priest, a Levite, an Israelite.

כ"מ = כבוד מעלתך your honourable rank; כן מוכח thus it is argued or refuted; כן משמע thus it is understood; thus it appears; כסף משנה double money; N. B; כסף מזוקק refined silver N. B; כתר מלכות crown, kingdom (two attributes); the royal crown; N. B; כן מצאתי thus I found; כל מקום every place.

כ"מד = כמאן דאמר as what he says.

כמ"דא = כמו דאתאמר as it is said.

כמ"יל ל"בד = כי מלאכיו יצוה לך לשמרך בכל דרכיך for he shall give his angels charge over thee, to keep thee in all thy ways.

כ"מר = כבוד מעלת רבי the honourable rank of Rabbi—.

כ"מש = כמו שאמר or שכתב as he says or writes; כל מקום שנאמר every place where it is said.

כמ"שה = כמו שאמרו החכמים as the wise men say; כמו שהיה as it was.

כמ"של = כמו שאמר or שכתב למעלה as he says or writes above.

כ"מת = כבוד מעלת תפארתך your honourable and glorious rank.

כ"נ = כסף נבחר choice silver; N. B; כן נראה thus it appears.

כנ"הג or כ"נה = כנסת הגדולה the great Synod, Assembly or Synagogue.*

כ"נז = כנזכר as it is mentioned.

כנ"זל = כנזכר לעיל or למעלה as mentioned above.

כנז"למ = כנזכר למטה as mentioned below.

כ"ני = כנסת ישראל the congregation of Israel; the Jewish church; כנסת יחזקאל the assembly or synagogue of Ezekiel.

כ"נל = כן נראה לי thus it appears to me; כנזכר לעיל as mentioned above; כנזכר לקמן as mentioned below or within.

כ"ספ = כל סופי פסוקים all periods or full stops.

---

* This name is applied to the great Synod presided over by Ezra, and consisting of 120 members, and is alleged to have been engaged in restoring and reforming the worship of the Temple after the return of the Jews from Babylon.

כ"ע = כולי עלמא or כל עולם the whole world; כל ענין the whole subject or matter; כח עליון the highest or greatest Power; כתר עליון the highest crown; כדי עניבה by a slip knot.

כ"פ = כן פסק thus he decides; כל פעם every time; כל פנים all looks, modes, or reasons; כי פליגי if there be any difference of opinion; כלי פז a vessel of pure gold; N. B; כתונת פסים a coat of many colours; N. B.

כ"צ = כהן צדק the true priest; the priest of righteousness.

כ"צל = כן צריך להיות it ought to be so.

כ"ק = כל קריא the whole passage; כתבי קודש the Sacred Writings; the Holy Scripture.

כ"ש = כמו שאמר or שכתב as he says or writes; כמו שכתוב as it is written; כבוד שמו his honoured name; כל שכן much more so; כל שהוא all that may be; a little; כוונת שלמה the devotion or object of Solomon; N. B.

כ"שט = כתר שם טוב the crown of a good name.

כש"נע = כשהוא נקשר עם as it is joined or tied to.

כ"שת = כבוד שם תורתו the honour of his learned name; כבוד שם תפארתו the honour of his glorious name.

כ"ת = כבוד תפארתו the honour of his glory; כתר תורה the crown of the Law.

כת"חזל = כתקון חכמים זכרונם לברכה as ordained by wise men of blessed memory.

כ"תי = כן תרגם יונתן thus translates Jonathan.

אות ל

ל״ stands for 30; as a sign of the dative, to, for; also for לשון tongue or language.

ל״א = לשון אחד one language; לשון אחר another word or language; לשון אחרים the language or saying of others; לשון אשכנז the German language; למד אלף a quiescent verb having א for its third radical.

ל״אא = לאדני אבי to or of my honoured father.

לא״וא = לכל אחד ואחד to each and every one.

ל״אי = לאורך ימים to the utmost length of days; לארץ ישראל to the land of Israel.

ל״אימ = לאורך ימים טובים for many happy days; for a long happy life.

ל״אל = לא אליכם may it not be to you.

ל״ב = לישנא בתרא the latter language or saying.

לב״ע = לבריאת עולם to or of the creation of the world.

ל״ג = לא גרסינן we do not read; לית גרסא there is no reading.

לג״לע = שלשה ושלשים לעומר thirty third day of Omer.

ל״ד = לית דכותיה there is no parallel to it; לא דמי it is not like; לדוד to or of David; לאו דוקא not only; לחם דמעה a sorrowful bread; N. B.

לד״א = לדעת אונקלוס according to the opinion of Onkelos.

לד"אע = לדעת אבן עזרא according to the opinion of Eben Ezra.

ל"די = לדעת יונתן according to the opinion of Jonathan.

ל"דק = לדרך קבלה according to the Kabbala; or tradition; לדעת קמחי according to the opinion of Kimchi; לדעת קצת according to the opinion of some; לא דמיא קריאתו its reading has no parallel.

ל"דת = לדין תורה according to the judgment or rule of the Law.

ל"ה = לייי to God; למען השם for God's sake; לימא הכי he ought to have said so; למד הא a quiescent verb having ה for its third radical.

ל"הד = למה הדבר דומה what is this thing like.

ל"הפ = לחם הפנים the shew bread; N. B.

ל"הק = לשון הקודש the holy language i. e. Hebrew; לקט הקמח gleaning of the flour; N. B.

ל"הר = לשון הרע slander.

ל"ו = לעולם ועד for ever and ever.

ל"ז = לשון זה this language; this saying; לשון זכר a word of the masculine gender.

ל"זא = לזאת אמר for this he says.

ל"ח = לחודש of the month; לשון חכמים Rabbanical language; לחם חמודות costly or pleasant bread; N. B; למצא חן to find favour.

ל"חא = לחם אבירים princely food; N. B.

לח״ולח = לחן ולחסד to (grant) favour and mercy.

לחט״ול = לחיים טובים ולשלום to a happy and peaceful life.

ל״חמ = לחם משנה double bread; N. B.

ל״ט = לקח טוב a good doctrine; N. B.

ל״י = לשנה יתירה for or of the additional year; לקט יוסף the gleaning of Joseph N. B; לחם יהודה the bread of Judah; N. B; לשון יחיד a word of the singular number.

ל״יו = ליונתן of or to Jonathan.

ל״יח = ליוצאי חלציו to those who come out of his loins; to his descendants.

לי״לו = לא יכבה לעולם ועד may it not be extinguished for ever.

לי״קבה = לשם יחוד קודשא בריך הוא in the name of the unity of the Holy and Blessed One; in the singular name of the Holy and Blessed One.

ל״ית = ליקוטי תורה gleanings or extracts from the Law.

ל״כא = לכן אמר therefore he says; לכל אחד o every one.

ל״כמ = לכבוד מעלתך to your honourable rank.

ל״כנ = לכך נאמר for this it is said; for this we say.

ל״כע = לכולי עלמה according to the general opinion.

ל״ל = לויה לדרך accompanying one to a short distance of his journey ; לשון למודים the language of the learned ; the practised tongue ; ליכא למימר there is none to say or saying ; לעתיד לבא for or in the future; למה לי why to me? why have I ? למה ליה why to him? why has he &c.

ל"מ = לשון מקרא language of the Scripture ; לחם משנה double bread ; N. B ; לא מבעיא not required ; not asked ; not questioned.

למ"בי = למספר בני ישראל according to the number of the children of Israel.

ל"מד = למן דאמר to him who says.

למ"זט = למזל טוב for good luck.

ל"מכ = למעלת כבודך to your honourable rank.

למ"כת = למעלת כבוד תורתו to the honourable rank of his learning.

ל"נ = לכן נאמר therefore it is said ; therefore we say ; לי נראה to me it appears ; לשון נקבה a word of the feminine gender.

ל"ס = לחם סתרים hidden bread ; N. B.

ל"סי = לפורקנך סברית יי for thy salvation do I hope, O Lord.

ל"עד = לעניות דעתי to my poor knowledge.

לע"והב = לעולם הבא in the world to come.

ל"עז = לשון עם זר the language of a strange people.

ל"עט = לב עין טחול heart, eye, spleen.

לע"יט = לערב יום טוב for the eve of a holiday.

ל"על = לעתיד לבא for or in the future.

לע"ע = לעת עתה for this time; לעולמי עד for everlasting.

לע"תל = לעתיד לבוא for or in the future.

ל"פ = לפלוני to so and so; לית פליג there is no disagreement in it; למד פעל the third letter of the root; ליקוטי פרדס gleanings in a garden N. B.

ל"פג = לפרט גדול of great reckoning including thousands.

לפ"וד = לפום דינא according to the law.

ל"פז = לפום זה or לפי זה according to this.

ל"פי = לפיכך therefore; לפירוש יונתן of or according to the translation of Jonathan.

לפ"עד = לפי עניות דעתי according to my poor knowledge.

ל"פק = לפרט קטן of small reckoning, omitting thousands.

ל"צ = לא צריך not required.

ל"ק = לא קרי not read; לא קשה not difficult; לא קשיא not disputed or argued; לישנא קמא former language or saying; לשון קצר short language or few words.

ל"קי = לישועתך קויתי יי for thy salvation do I wait, O Lord.

לק"מ = לא קשה מדי there is nothing difficult, it is not to be disputed at all; there is nothing to be disputed.

לק"ש = ליקוטי שושנים gleanings of lilies; N. B.

ל"ר = לשון רבים a word of the plural number; לחם רב much bread; N. B.

ל"ש = לא שייך not suitable; לא שנא he did not teach; לחם שלמה the bread of Solomon; N. B.

לש"ו = ליקוטי שכחה ופאה gleanings or extracts from the rules relating to the sheaf forgotten in the field and the corner of the field; N. B. *

ל"שש = לשם שמים for the name of God.

ל"ת = לא תעשה thou shalt not do; a negative precept; לבוש תכלת a purple dress; N. B.

ל"תא = לא תמעד אשוריו his footsteps shall not totter.

אות מ

מ" stands for 40; at the beginning of words for from; than; also for מור lord; מרת lady; (terms of respect to an elder relation); מלכות kingdom; מדרש college; allegorical exposition.

מ"א = משקל אחד one or same weight; one or same grammatical form; משקל אחר another weight; another grammatical form; מין אחד one kind; מדרש אגדה an allegorical narration; מערכות אלהים armies of God; N. B; מפעלות אלהים works of God; N. B. מטה אהרון the rod of Aaron; N. B. מגן אברהם the shield of Abraham; N. B; מתיר אסורים He who sets

* See Ex. xix 9, 10; and Deut. xxiv. 19—21.

prisoners at liberty; מים אחרונים last water;* מקום אחר another place.

מא"בח = מור אליהו בן חיים the honoured Elijah the son of Haeem.

מא"ז = מאור זרוע a sown luminary; N. B.

מ"אל = מנא אמינא ליה whence have we said to him; whence have we said it; מאי איכא למימר what is there to be said.

מ"אס = מאין סוף from the Infinite.

מאר"זל = מאמר רבותינו זכרונם לברכת the saying of our Rabbies of blessed memory.

מ"ב = מנחה בלולה a mingled offering; N. B. מעשה בראשית the work of creation, a description of the beginning or creation; משאת בנימן the portion of Benjamin; N. B. מסעות בנימן the travels of Benjamin; N. B.; מדבר בעדו one speaking of himself; the first person in grammar.

מ"בו = מלך בשר ודם a human king.

מב"יא = מתן בסתר יכפה אף a secret gift appeases anger.

מ"בס = מנחם בן סרוק Menahem the son of Seruk.

מב"עי = מבעוד יום while it is yet the day.

מ"בת = מנשים באהל תברך blessed may she be above women in the tent (a phrase used after the name of a female).

מ"ג = מגזרה by decree; מספר גדול a great number

* Water for washing hands after a meal is called last water.

greater calculation i. e. counting units as tens, hundreds &c; מחזור גדול the great or solar cycle; מסורה גדולה the great Masora; N. B; מנחה גדולה a great present; N. B.

מ״גא = מגלת אסתר the book of Esther; מגן אברהם the Shield of Abraham; N. B; מגן אבות the Shield of the patriarchs; N. B.

מג״אר = מגיני ארץ shields i.e, princes of the earth; N.B.

מג״דד = מגדל דוד דרשות Lectures called Migdal David; i. e. the tower of David; N. B.

מ״גס = מגלת סתרים a scroll of mysteries; N. B.

מ״גע = מגלה עמוקות the revealer of deep or hidden things; N. B; מגן עדן from the garden of Eden; מחיה גפן עץ food, vine, (fruit of) a tree *

מ״גש = מגיני שלמה the shields of Solomon; N.B; מגזרה שוה by analogy.

מ״גת = מגלת תענית a tract of the Talmud on fasts; מלכות גבורה תפארת kingdom, power, beauty.

מ״ד = מאן דאמר he who says; מאי דכתיב what is it that is written; what is the meaning of the words or passage; מיין דוכרין male waters; מהו דתימא what is it that you say; מדרש a college; an allegorical exposition; מגן דוד the Shield of David; N. B; מלא דרשות full of discourses.

מד״א = מה דאתאמר what is said.

מד״הד = מדת הדין the attribute of justice.

* After eating these a particular grace is to be said.

מד"הר = מדת הרחמים the attribute of mercy.

מד"ר = מדרש רבא an allegorical exposition of Law and the five Megilloth.

מ"ה = מיי or מהשם from God; מאור הגולה the light of the captivity; משום הכי on such account; in the name of such; מדת הדין the attribute of justice; מלאך המות the angel of death; מלאכי השרת the ministering angels; מדת העולם extent of the world; usage of the world; מלכי האומות heathen kings; מבקשי יי those who seek God; מדרש הנעלם the hidden exposition; N. B; מנות הלוי portions of the Levite N. B; משמרת הבית watching the house; N. B.; מכריז החודש one who proclaims the new moon.

מ"הג = מהלכות גזילה or גניבה from the laws of robbery or theft.

מה"חול = מהחותם למטה from the undersigned.

מ"הט = מוריד הטל He who sends the dew.

מ"הל = מאת המוציא לאור from the publisher.

מ"המ = מהלכות מכירה from the laws of sale; מהלכות מלוה from the laws of loan; מלאך המות the angel of death.

מה"מא = מהלכות מאכלות אסורות from the laws of forbidden food.

מהמ"דתר = מנא הני מילי דתנו רבנן whence or how are these words, which our Rabbies teach, applicable.

מה"נמ = מהלכות נזיקי ממון from the laws of the loss of money.

מ"הס = מהר סיני from or on Mount Sinai.

מ"הע = מכתב העתי a newspaper.

מ"הר or **מהרר** or **מוהרר** = מורנו הרב רבי our honoured and learned Rabbi.

מהר"אי = מורנו הרב רבי איסרלש our honoured and learned Rabbi Isrelash.

מה"ראמ = מורנו הרב רבי אליהו מזרחי our honoured and learned Rabbi Elyahoo Mizrahee.

מה"ראש = מורנו הרב רבי אהרון ששון our honoured and learned Rabbi Aaron Sason.

מה"רחו = מורנו הרב רבי חיים ויטאל our honoured and learned Rabbi Haeem Wital.

מה"רחש = מורנו הרב רבי חיים שבתי our honoured and learned Rabbi Haeem Shabbethai.

מח"ריא = מורנו חרב רבי יצהק אבוהב our honoured and learned Rabbi Isaac Abuhab.

מהריבל = מורנו הרב רבי יוסף בן לב our honoured and learned Rabbi Joseph the son of Leb.

מה"ריו = מורנו הרב רבי יעקב ווייל our honoured and learned Rabbi Jacob Wawayal.

מה"ריט = מורנו הרב רבי יוסף טראני our honoured and learned Rabbi Joseph Taranee.

מהר"יטצ = מורנו הרב רבי יום טוב צהלון our honoured and learned Rabbi Yom Tob Sahlon.

מה"ריל = מרנו הרב רבי יעקב לוי our honoured and learned Rabbi Jacob Levi; מורנו הרב רבי יצחק לוריא our honoured and learned Rabbi Isaac Luria.

מה"ריק = מורנו הרב רבי יוסף קארו our honoured and learned Rabbi Joseph Karoo; מרנו הרב רבי יוסף קולון our honoured and learned Rabbi Joseph Kolon.

מהר"לבח = מרנו הרב רבי לוי בן חביב our honoured and learned Rabbi Levi the son of Chabib.

מה"רמא = מורנו הרב רבי משה איסרלש our honoured and learned Rabbi Moses Isrelash.

מהר"מט = מורנו הרב רבי משה טראני our honoured and learned Rabbi Moses Taranee.

מהר"מי = מורנו הרב רבי מרדכי יפה our honoured and learned Rabbi Mordecai Yaphe.

מהר"ממ = מורנו הרב רבי מאיר מפדווא our honoured and learned Rabbi Meir of Padua.

מהר"מע = מורנו הרב רבי מנחם עזריה our honoured and learned Rabbi Menahem Azariah.

מה"רע = מו,נו הרב רבי עוזר our honoured and learned Rabbi Ozer.

מהר"רח = מורנו הרב רבי חיים ויטל our honoured and learned Rabbi Haeem Weetal.

מה"רשא = מורנו הרב רבי שלמה אדלש our honoured and learned Rabbi Solomon Edlash.

מה"רשך = מורנו הרב רבי שלמה כהן our honoured and learned Rabbi Solomon Cohen.

מה"רשל = מורנו הרב רבי שלמה לוריא our honoured and learned Rabbi Solomon Luria.

מ"הש = מהלכות שחיטה from the laws of slaughtreing animals ; מלאכי השרת the ministering angels.

מ״הת = מהלכות תפלה from the laws of prayer.

מה״תת = מהלכות תלמוד תורה from the laws of the study of the Law.

מ״וח = מור חמי my honoured father-in-law.

מו״כד or **מ״כד** = מוביל כתב דנא the bearer of this letter.

מ״ול = מוציא לאור a publisher.

מ״ומ = מוקדם ומאוחר transposition ; מעתה ומעכשיו from now and henceforth ; משא ומתן buying and selling ; trade.

מ״ונ = מורה נבוכים a guide for the perplexed ; N. B.

מ״וצ = מורה צדק an upright teacher.

מ״ז = משכב זכור sodomy.

מ״זט = מזל טוב a good luck.

מ״זי = מזבח יעקב Jacob's altar ; N. B.

מ״ח = מעין חכמה the spring or source of wisdom; N. B; מקור חיים fountain of life ; N. B; משנת הסידים the teaching of pious men; מעשה חייה the work or story of Chiyah.

מח״הש = מהצית השקל half a shekel.

מח״זל = מאמר הכמנו זכרונם לברכה the saying of our wise men of blessed memory.

מ״חנ = משלם הצי נזק paying half damage.

מ״ט = מאי טעמא or מה טעם what is the reason or

object; מזל טוב a good luck; מעשים טובים good works; מעשה טוביה the story or work of Tobiyah.

מ"טד = מטה דן the tribe of Dan; N. B.

מ"טי = מטה יוסף the tribe of Joseph; N. B.

מ"טמ = מטה משה the rod of Moses; N. B.

מ"י = מנא ידעינן whence do we know or understand; מלחמות יי the wars of God; מדבר יהודה the desert of Judah; N. B; מנחת יהודה the offering of Judah; N. B; מנחת יעקב the offering of Jacob; N. B.

מ"יט = מלבושי יום טוב dress for holidays.

מ"כ = מעלת כבודך your honourable rank; מנחת כהן the offering of a priest; N. B; מתנות כהונה the gifts of priesthood; N. B; מצאתי כתוב I found it written; מסכת כלה a tract of the Talmud called the Bride.

מכ"או = מכל אחד ואחד from each and every one.

מכ"בי = מי כמוך באלים יי who is like unto thee, O Lord, among Gods.

מ"כד = מוביל כתב דנא the bearer of this letter.

מ"כי = מכירת יוסף the sale of Joseph.

מ"כל = מכתם לדוד a golden Psalm of David; N. B.

מ"כע = מכתבי עתים newspapers.

מ"כש = מכל שכן much more, much less.

מ"כת = מעלת כבוד תפארתך your elevated and glorious rank.

מ"ל = מנא לן whence have we; מוציא לאור a publisher; מיבעי ליה it requires; מזמור לתודה a Psalm of praise; N. B.; מצרף לכסף a purifier of silver; N. B.

מ"לה = מלכות הרשעה the kingdom of wickedness.

מל"הד = משל למה הדבר דומה for example, to what does this word refer; for example, what is this thing like.

מ"לת = מצות לא תעשה a negative precept.

מ"מ = מכל מקום at all events; at any rate; מורה מקום a pointer, a reference; מעשה מרכבה the description of the divine chariot mentioned in Eze. I; מאי משמע what do we understand; מצות מת the duty or merit of attending a funeral; מלעה מעלה higher and higher; מטה מטה lower and lower; מעלה מטה more or less; מטה משה the rod of Moses; N. B.

ממ"דהי or **מ"מה** = ממדינת הים from the regions of the sea.

מ"מהמ = מלך מלכי המלכים the Supreme King of Kings.

מ"מנ = ממה נפשך in whatever way you wish.

מ"מש = שאמר or ממה שכתב from what he wrote or said.

מ"נ = ממה נפשך in whatever way you wish; משיבת נפש restoration of life; מאורות נתן the luminaries of Nathan; N. B; מיין נוקבין female waters: מורה נבוכים a guide for the perplexed; N. B.

מ״נה = מנות הלוי portions of the Levite; N. B.

מנ״וה = מנורת המאור a candlestick for light; N.B.

מ״נל = מנא נפקא לן whence is it produced for us; whence do we find it.

מ״נש = משלם נזק שלם one paying the whole damage.

מנ״שב = מחמשים שערי בינה from the fifty gates of understanding.

מ״ס = מספר from the book; number; מסכת a tract; מר סבר a teacher thinks; מגילת סתרים the scroll of secrets; מגילת ספר the scroll of a book; מסכת סופרים the tract on scribes; מוחא סתימאה the closed brain.

מ״סג = מסורה גדולה the great Masora; N. B.

מס״דא = מסכת דרך ארץ the tract on politeness or mannerly behaviour.

מס״לת = מסיח לפי תומו one speaking unintentionally.

מ״סק = מסורה קטנה the small Masora; N. B.

מ״ע = מצות עשה an affirmative precept; מאור עינים light of the eyes; a friendly countenance; מגלה עמוקות revealer of hidden things; מכתב עתי a newspaper; מנחם עזריה Menahem Azariah; N. B.; מגדל עז the tower of strength.

מ״עה = מעשה יי the work of God.

מע"הכ = מעלה עליו הכתוב he is considered in Scripture.

מ"עח = מספר עץ חיים from the book called עץ חיים the tree of life; מעין חכמה the fountain of wisdom; N. B; מעשה חכמים the work of wise men.

מ"עט = מעשים טובים good works.

מ"עי = מעבר יבק the ford of Jabbok; N. B.

מע"כת = מעלת כבוד תורתך the elevated character of your learning.

מ"על = מעת לעת from time to time; מלוה על פה lending verbally i. e. without any writing.

מ"עמ = מעדני מלך royal dainties; N. B.

מ"עס = מעולפת ספרים a thing overlaid with sapphires; N. B.

מע"הכ = מעלה עליו הכתוב he is considered in Scripture.

מ"עצ = מעגלי צדק paths of righteousness; right paths; N. B.

מ"עק = מאמר עולם קטן a discourse on the theory of microcosm.

מ"ער = מערכת an host; an army.

מע"שח = מעשה חייא the story or work of Hiyah

מע"שי בי"צו = מגדל עז שם יי בו ירוץ צדיק ונשגב the name of the Lord is a strong tower, the righteous runneth into it and is safe.

מ"עת = מעלת תפארתך your elevated glory.

מ"פ = מצע פסוק the middle of a sentence.

מ"פח = מפשר חלמין the interpreter of dreams.

מ"פע = מפי עליון from the mouth of the Most High.

מפ"רת = מפרש רבינו תם our Rabbi Tam explains.

מ"צ = מורה צדק an upright teacher; משפט צדק an upright judgment; מראה צבאות the sight or vision of hosts; N. B; משפטי צדק upright judgments; N. B.

מ"ק = מועד קטן a minor festival; a tract in the Talmud; מקרא קודש a holy convocation; מספר קטן a small number; units; smaller calculation i.e. counting tens and hundreds as units; מחזור קטן the smaller or lunar cycle;

מק"ח = מקור חיים the fountain of life.

מק"חד = מקור חיים דרשות discourses called מקור חיים

מק"חשע = מקור חיים שלחן ערוך a commentary on שלחן ערוך called מקור חיים

מ"קק = מקראי קודש holy convocations.

מ"ר = מורי רבי my master (and) my teacher; מדרש רות the allegorical exposition of the book of Ruth; מורת רוח grief of mind; משה רבינו our master Moses; מדרש רבה the allegorical exposition of the Law and the five Megilloth; מדת רחמים the attribute of mercy.

מר"א = משנת רבי אליעזר the Mishna or teaching of Rabbi Eliezer.

מר"ה = מראות הצובאות adorners' looking-glasses; מראש השנה from the new year.

מר"כה = מרכבת המשנה the second chariot; N.B.

מ"רל = מרפה לנפש a cure for the soul; מה רצונו לומר what does he wish or mean to say.

מ"רן = מאתים רבנים נסמך certified by two hundred Rabbies.

מר"עה = משה רבינו עליו השלום Moses our master may peace be on him.

מ"ש = מדרש שמואל the school of Samuel; the allegorical exposition of Samuel; N. B.; מצות שמורים Passover breads prepared from wheat carefully preserved; N. B; מוצאי שבת the close of Sabbath; מה שכתב or שאמר what he says or writes; מי שכתב or שאמר he who says or writes; מה שכתוב what is written; מאי שנא what does it teach; משפטי שמואל the judgments of Samuel; N. B.

מ"שה = מה שאמר הכתוב what the Scripture says; what the writing says.

מש"כ = מה שכתוב what is written; מה שאין כן what is not so.

מ"שק = מוצאי שבת קודש the close of the holy Sabbath.

מש"רזל = מה שאמרו רבותינו זכרונם לברכה what our Rabbies of blessed memory say.

מ״ת = מתן תורה the gift of the Law ; משנה תורה a copy of the Law ; מכחישי תורה those who deny the truth of the Law ; infidels.

אות נ

נ״ stands for 50 ; at the beginning of verbs as the characterestic prefix of Niphal ; as first person plural common future ; at the end as third person plural feminine ; also for בן son.

נ״א = נוסח אחר or נוסחא אחרינא another version; נא אדני I pray, O lord ; נשמת אדם the soul of man ; N. B ; נחלת אבות an inheritance from the fathers ; N. B.

נ״אח = נסוג אחור drawing or holding back.

נ״ב = נות ביתך she who dwells in your house ; the beauty of your house ; your wife ; נכתב בצדו written on its side ; נחלת בנימן the inheritance of Benjamin ; N. B.

נ״בת = נפשו בעדן תנוח may his soul rest in Eden.

נ״ד = נראה דברו his word becomes clear.

נד״י = נדחי ישראל the outcasts of Israel.

נ״ה = נזר הקודש the holy mitre ; נצח הוד triumph, glory.

נ״הי = נצח הוד יסוד triumph, glory, basis.

נ״וא = נדב ואביהו Nadab and Abihu, the sons of Aaron.

נ״וע ארק שדש = נחמו׳ ותאמר ציון׳ עניה סוערה׳ אנכי אנכי׳ רני עקרה׳ קומי אורי׳ שוש אשיש׳

דרשו יי · שובה ישראל · this abbreviation shows the Haftaroth of the Sabbaths that fall between the Day of Lamentation and the Day of Atonement, and of the fast of Gedaliah. The first seven are of consolation; and the last two, for צום גדליה and שבת תשובה, are of repentance.

נ״וק = נוקבא female.

נ״זי = נעים זמירות ישראל the pleasant songs or music of the Israelites; the sweet Psalmist or David; a competent Chazan ; N. B.

נ״ח = נר חנוכה the lamp of the Feast of Dedication; נפש חיים a living soul ; N. B; נפש חכמה a wise soul ; N. B.

נ״חי = נחלת יעקב the inheritance of Jacob ; N. B.

נח״לא = נחי למד אלף a quiescent verb having א for its third radical.

נח״לה = נחי למד הא a quiescent verb having ה for its third radical.

נח״ר = נחת רוח gratification to the spirit.

נח״ש - נחלת שבעה the inheritance of seven nations; N. B. נדוי חרם שמתא Niddui, Cherem, Shematta, three kinds of excommunications, one severer than the other.

נ״ט = נותן טעם one who gives a reason; that which gives taste

נ״טי = נטילת ידים washing hands.

נ״י = נפוצות יהודה the dispersed of Judah ; נרו יאיר He will light his lamp, a complimentary phrase used after the name of a person; נר ישראל the lamp of Israel; נטילת ידים washing hands; נימוקי יוסף annotations by Joseph.

נ״יש = נצח ישראל (God) the glory of Israel.

נ״כ = נביאים כתובים the Prophetical writings and the Hagiographa.

נ״ל = למעלה or נזכר לעיל the abovementioned; נראה לי it appears to me; נוכל לומר we can say; נפקא לן we infer; נר למאור a lamp for light.

נל״בע = נפטר לבית עולמו who (died or) left for his eternal home; נתבקש לבית עולמו who (died or) was sought for his eternal home.

נלי״שמ = נתבקש לישיבה של מעלה who (died or) was sought for the assembly of wise men above.

נל״לע = נוסף ללא ענין added without being required by the context; added without any purpose.

נל״לצ = נוסף ללא צורך added unnecessarily.

נ״מ = נפקא מניה we infer from it; hence it follows; נר מצוה the commandment is a lamp; נכסי מלוג paraphernalia; property brought by a bride beyond her dowry.

נ״נ = נעשה נבלה it becomes a carcass or forbidden for food.

נ״נס = נח נסתר a syllable, the last consonant of which is silent.

נ״נר = נח נראה a syllable, the last consonant of which is sounded.

נ״סו = נצח סלה ועד for ever, ever and ever.

נ״ע = נוחו עדן may his rest be in the Garden of Eden; a phrase used after the name of a deceased person; נגידי עם the rulers or leaders of the people.

נ״עו = נחי עין ואו a quiescent verb having ו for its second radical.

נ״עח = נוף עץ חיים the volume called עץ חיים

נ״פא = נפילת אפים falling prostrate on the face in daily prayers; נחי פא אלף a quiescent verb having א for its first radical.

נ״פי = נחי פא יוד a quiescent verb having י for its first radical.

נ״צ = נחלת צבי the inheritance of the glorious land; נחמת ציון the consolation of Zion; נופת צופים a honeycomb; N. B.

נ״צב = נכסי צאן ברזל property like sheep considered as iron.

נ״ק = נקרא we read; we call; he or it is called.

נק״הכ = נקודות הכסף studs of silver; N. B.

נ״רו = נטרה רחמנא ופרקיה may the Merciful protect and save him; נטרה רחמנא וברכיה may the Merciful protect and bless him; נטרה רחמנא ויחייהו may the Merciful protect him and grant him long life; נוצרו רם ונשא his Protector is high and exalted.

נ״רן = נפש רוח נשמה life, spirit, soul.

נר״נח = נפש רוח נשמה היה life, spirit, soul, breath.

נ״ש = נוה שלום the dwelling of peace; נזק שלם full damage; נימוקי שמואל annotations of Samuel; נחלת שבעה the inheritance of the seven aboriginal nations of the Holy Land; N. B.

נ״שב = חמישים שערי בינה the fifty gates of understanding.

נ״שר = נפתלי שבע רצון Naphtali is satisfied with favours; N. B.

נ״ת = נורא תהלות fearful in praises; N. B; נתינת תורה the giving of the Law.

נת״בע = נוחה תהיה בגן עדן or נוחו may his or her rest be in Eden; a phrase used after the name of a deceased person.

אות ס

ס״ stands for 60; also for ספר a book; סימן a chapter; an omen; a sign; סתומה closed; closely written; סעיף a section.

ס״א = ספר אחר another book; ספרים אחרים other books; סבה אחת one cause; סימן אחר another chapter; another sign; סעיף ראשון section first; סטרא אחרא the spirit opposed to virtue or holiness; סברא אחרינא another opinion; ספרי אמונה books of faith.

ס״אח = ספר אורחות חיים a book called אורחות חיים the ways of life.

ס״ב = סלת בלולה mingled flour; N. B; סעיף שני section second &c.

ס"ג = סוף גמרא the end of Gemara-; ספר גלגולים a book on spheres or transmigration of souls ; סדר גט the order or manner of divorce.

ס"ד = ספרא דצניעותא the book of secrets ; a book on modesty; סלקא דעתך do you suppose? סוף דבר the end of a thing ; at last ; סעדא דשמיה the help of God.

ס"דא = סלקא דעתך אמינא do you suppose our saying (to be correct)?

ס"דה = סדר היום the prayer and portions of the Scripture &c. prescribed for the day.

ס"דצ = ספרא דצניעותא the book of secrets ; a book on modesty.

ס"ה = ספר הזהר the book of Zohar or splendour ; ספר היראה the book on the fear of God ; ספר הישר the book of Jasher ; סדר היום the prayer and portions of Scripture &c. prescribed for the day סך הכל the total sum.

ס"הב = סימן הבנין the sign or characterestic of the conjugation.

ס"הד = סדר הדורות a series of generations (an historical work).

ס"הז = ספר הזהר the book of Zohar or splendour.

ס"הח = ספר החרדים the book of Quakers ; N. B.

ס"הכ = ספר הכוונות the book of devotions ; N. B.

ס"המ = סימן המשקל the sign of the inflection ; סימן המין the sign of the gender.

ס"הע = ספירת העומר the numbering of the Omer.*

סו"ד = סוף דבר the end of a thing; at last.

ס"ז = ספר זכרונות a chronicle'; N. B.

ס"ח = סם חיים nectar; ספר חסידים the book of pious men; סדר חליצה the order or manner of release given to the widow of a deceased brother, who dies childless.

ס"ט = סימן טוב an auspicious omen; סופי טוב may my end be good.

ס"טא = סטרא אחרא the spirit opposed to virtue or holiness

ס"י = סימן a sign; an omen; a chapter; ספר יצירה the book of device or creation; N. B; ספר ישראל the book of Israel; N. B.

ס"יו = ספר יוחסין the book of geneologies (an historical work).

סי"לטי = סיפיה לטובה יהיה may his or its end be for good.

ס"ל = סבירה ליה he is of opinion.

ס"לה = סב למעלה השר turn above singer; סימן לשנות הקול a sign to change the voice.

ס"מ = ספר מוסר the book of morals; N. B.; סמאל the angel of death.

ס"מג = ספר מצות גדול the larger book of precepts.

* The numbering of forty nine days from the Second Day of Passover to the Feast of Weeks is called the numbering of the Omer.

ס"מי = ספר מלחמות יי the book of the wars of God.

ס"מע = ספר מאירת עינים the book called מאירת עינים enlightening of the eyes.

ס"מק = ספר מצות קטן the smaller book of precepts.

ס"מר = ספר מצות רמבם the book of precepts by Maimonides

ס"ס = סוף סימן the end of chapter—; סוף סוף the perfect end of a matter; ספק ספיקא the slightest doubt.

ס"ע = סדר עולם the chronicle of the world; N. B; סדר עבודה the manner of worship.

ס"עא = סוף עמוד ראשון the end of the first page or column.

ס"פ = סוף פרק the end of chapter—; סוף פסוק a tonic accent at the end of a sentence equal to a period; סוף פרשה the end of a section of the Law read on a Sabbath day; סוד פסוק the mystery of a sentence.

ס"פא = סוף פרוטה אחרונה to the last farthing.

ס"פק = סוף פרק קמא the end of the first chapter.

ס"ק = סעיף קטן a small branch; a small section; ספק קדושין doubt of betrothal.

ס"ר = סבה ראשונה The First Cause; God.

סר"נכ = סמיכות רבוי נקבה כנוי construct state, plural number, feminine gender, pronoun.

ס״שר = ספר שמות רבה the allegorical exposition of the book of Exodus.

ס״ת = ספר תורה the book of the Law; סתרי תורה mysteries of the Law; סופי תיבות final letters.

ס״תר = סוף תוך ראש end, middle, beginning.

אות ע

ע״ stands for 70;also for עמוד page or column; ערך order or arrangement; ערב the eve of.

ע״א = עמוד ראשון first page or column; ענין אחד one subject or matter; ענין אחר another subject or matter; עוד אחר still another one; עוד אחד one more; עבודת אלילים the worship of idols; עובדי אלילים worshippers of idols; עולם אצילה the world of emanation; עוללות אפרים the gleaning of the grapes of Ephraim.

עא״כו = על אחת כמה וכמה instead of one, how many more.

ע״ב = עבודת בורא the worship of the Creator; עיר בנימן a city of Benjamin; עולם בריאה the world of creation; עולת בקר a morning sacrifice; עמק ברכה the vale of blessing; עמוד שני the second page or column &c.

ע״בג = עם בן or בת גילה with the delightful son or daughter.

ע״בי = עד בלי ירח until the moon fades; as long as the moon lasts.

עב"רי = עיין ברכי יוסף see the book called ברכי יוסף Joseph's knees.

ע"ג = על גב or על גבי on the back of; generally the prepositions on, upon, over.

עג"הק = על גבי הקרקה on the surface of the ground.

ע"ד = על דבר on account of; על דרך by the way of; על דא on this; על דעת according to the opinion of; עניות דעתי my poor knowledge; עיר דוד the city of David; עתיקא דעתיקין The Most Ancient; God.

ע"דה = על דרך האמת or על דרך האמתי in truth.

ע"דז = על דבר זה on account of this; על דרך זה by this way.

ע"דמ = על דרך משל for example; figuratively; על דבר מה on account of what; on some account.

ע"דש = על דרך שלום in or by a peaceful way.

ע"ה = עולת התמיד the continual burnt offering; N.B; עליה השלום or עליו peace be unto him or her;* עליהם or עליהן השלום peace be unto them; ענין הזה this subject or matter; עמק המלך the king's vale; N. B; עבודת המלך the service of the king; עין הקורא the eye of the reader; עמי הארץ or עם people of the land; illiterate person or persons; עם המלה with the word; עזר השם the help of God; עבד השם the servant of God; עם האותיות with the letters; עמק הברכה the vale of blessing; עומק הלכה the obscurity of the

* These phrases are used after the names of deceased persons.

rule; ערוגת הבושם a bed of spices; עולם הנפשות the world of spirits; עמוד השחר the pillar of dawn or morning; עם הכולל with the whole.

עו"הב or **ע"הב** = עולם הבא the future world.

ע"הג = עבודת הגרשוני the service of the Gershonite; N. B.

עו"הז or **עהז** = עולם הזה this world.

עה"ח = על החתום about the signatures or seals.

ע"הק = עבודת הקודש the holy worship; עיר הקודש the Holy City.

ע"הר = עין הרע the evil eye.

ע"הת = עם התיבה with the word.

ע"ז = עם זה with this; על זה on or about this; עמודיה שבעה its seven pillars; N. B.; עבודה זרה strange worship or idolatry; עטרת זקנים the crown of the old; N. B.

ע"זא = על זה אמר on or about this he says.

ע"זנ = על זה נאמר on or about this it is said.

ע"ח = עץ חיים the tree of life.

ע"חמ = עדים חתומי מטה the undersigned witnesses.

ע"י = על יד through; by; על ידי by means of; עולת יצחק the burnt offering of Isaac; N. B; עין יעקב the eye or fountain of Jacob; N. B.; עמק יהושפט the vale of Jehoshaphat; N. B.; עתיק יומין The Ancient of Days; God.

ע״הכ = ערב יום הכפורים the eve of the Day of Atonement.

ע״י = עין יוסף the eye or fountain of Joseph; N. B.

ע״ז = על ידי זה by means of this.

ע״ט = ערב יום טוב the eve of a holiday.

ע״כ = ערב יום כפור the eve of the Day of Atonement.

ע״ל = עמק יהושפט לקוטים extracts called עמק יהושפט

ע״מ = על ידי מוקדם by means of the former or foregoing; עיר מקלט a city of refuge; עיני משה the eyes of Moses; N. B.

ע״קות = עיר קודשינו ותפארתינו our holy and glorious city.

ע״ש = עין ישראל the eye or fountain of Israel; N. B.

ע״ת = עיר תהלה the celebrated city.

ע״כ = על כן therefore; על כל on all; עד כאן so far; until here; על כרחו being compelled; עבודת כוכבים the worship of stars.

ע״כד = עד כאן דבריו so far are his words; על כל דא on or about all this.

ע״כום = עובדי כוכבים ומזלות the worshippers of stars and planets or the signs of Zodiac.

ע״כז = עם כל זה for all that.

ע״כל = עד כאן לשונו so far is what he says

עכ"מד = על כל מה דכתיב about all what is written.

עכ"פ = על כל פנים at all events; עד כאן פירושו so far is his explanation.

ע"כצ = על כל צד on every side.

ע"ל = עיין לעיל refer or consider above; עיין לקמן refer or consider below or within.

ע"מ = על משקל according to the weight; according to the grammatical form; עשרה מאמרות the ten sayings or commandments; על מנת on condition; עול משקץ the yoke of a worker of abomination or of an idolator; על מכבש on the press.

ע"מא = על משקל אחד according to one or the same weight; according to one or the same grammatical form.

עמי"עשו = עזרי מעם יי עושה שמים וארץ my help comes from the Lord, who made heaven and earth.

עמ"לפ = על מנת לקבל פרס for the sake of receiving a reward.

ע"מש = על מה שאמר or שכתב on or about what he says or writes; עמודי שש pillars of marble; N. B.; עד מאה שנים until a hundred years.

ע"נ = עליו נאמר it is said about him or it.

ע"נג = עדן נהר גן Eden, river, garden.

ע"ני = על נטילת ידים (blessing after) washing hands.

ע"ס = עד סוף to the end; עד סימן until chapter—; עשר ספירות the ten Sephiroth or attributes; עט סופר pen of a writer; ערב סכות the eve of the Feast of Tabernacles; עטור סופרים the removal of some letters from the text of the Scripture by the scribes.

עס"פא = עד סוף פרוטא אחרונא to the last farthing.

ע"ע = עבד עברי a Hebrew servant; עגלה ערופה the heifer whose neck is broken; עיין עליו refer or consider over it; עיין עוד look or consider again; עין עין a verb having the same letter for its second and third radicals.

ע"עא = עובדי עבודת אלילים the worshippers of idols.

ע"עז = עובדי עבודה זרה the worshippers of strange gods; the devotees of strange worship.

ע"עש = עיין עוד שם look or consider there again.

ע"פ = על פי by the command of—; according to—; על פני on the face of; עשרה פעמים ten times; ערב פסח the eve of the Feast of Passover; על פסוק on a certain sentence; על פרשה on a certain portion of the Law; עין פעל the second radical letter.

עפ"המ = על פי המסורת according to the Masoreth.

ע"פי = על פי יי by the command of God.

ע"צ = על צד on the side of—; עטרת צבי a crown of glory; N. B.

ע"צי = עצמות יוסף the bones of Joseph.

ע"ק = עוד קשה still more difficult; עתיקא קדישא

The Ancient and Holy One; God; ערב קבלן a security admitting the terms of an agreement.

ע״קו = עיר קדשנו ותפארתנו our holy and glorious city.

ע״קי = עקידת יצחק the binding or offering of Isaac; N. B.

ע״קל = עוד קשה לי still more difficult to me; he opposed me again.

ע״קק = עליית קיר קטנה a little chamber; N. B.

ע״ר = עסיס רמונים wine of pomegranates; N. B.

ע״רה = ערב ראש השנה the eve of a New Year.

ע״רח = ערב ראש חדש the eve of a New Moon

ע״ש = ערב שבת the eve of a Sabbath; ערב שבועות the eve of the Feast of Weeks; עיין שם refer or consider there; עם שלום with peace; with compliments; על שם in the name of—; על שפת on the bank of—; עמודיה שבעה its seven pillars; N. B.; עולת שבת the burnt offering of Sabbath; עדות שקר false evidence.

ע״שב = עיין שם באורך refer there for full particulars.

עש״ית = עשרה ימי תשובה the ten penitential days.

ע״שק = ערב שבת קודש the eve of the holy Sabbath.

ע״ת = עולת תמיד the continual burnt offering; N. B.; ערובי תחומין joining limits for Sabbath day's journey.

עתו"אבי = עיר תהלה ואם בישראל the celebrated city and mother town of Israel.

אות פ

פ" stands for 80; also for פרק chapter; פעמים times; פסוק a sentence or verse; פירש he explains; פרשה a portion or section of the Law; פתוחה open; openly written; פלוני such a one.

פ"א = פאה a corner; פרק ראשון chapter first; פרקי אבות chapters of the Fathers (on ethics), a tract of the Talmud; פרוש אחר another interpretation; פעם אחת once; פעם אחר again; פני אדם a man's face; N. B.; פני אריה a lion's face; N. B.; פא אלף a quiescent verb having א for its first radical.

פ"אז = פני אריה זוטא the smaller book called פני אריה a lion's face.

פ"אט = פרק אלו טרפיות the chapter of the Talmud commencing with the words אלו טרפיות*

פ"אמ = פרק אין מעמידין the chapter of the Talmud commencing with the words אין מעמידין

פ"אפ = פה אל פה face to face.

פ"ב = פרק שני chapter second &c; פרק בתרא the last chapter.

פ"בי = פליטת בית יהודה the escaped of the house of Judah; the deliverance of the house of Judah.

*Every chapter of the Talmud is thus named from its commencing words.

פ״בפ = פנים בפנים face to face; פלוני בן פלוני such a one the son of such a one.

פ״ג = פלוגתא גדולה a great part; פתח גנובה furtive Patha.

פגה = פרק גיד הנשה the chapter of the Talmud commencing with the words גיד הנשה

פג״יג = * פורץ גדר ישכנו נחש a serpant shall bite him, who breaks an hedge or trespasses a limit.

פ״ד = פתיחה דספרא the introduction or opening of a book; פסקא דספרא the division of a book.

פ״ה = פסוק הוא it is a passage from the Scripture; פרוש הפסוק the explanation of the sentence.

פ״הא = פתח האהל the door of the tabernacle.

פהב״עי = פרק הבא על יבמתו the chapter of the Talmud commencing with the words הבא על יבמתו

פ״ו = פריה ורביה increasing and multiplying by marriage.

פ״וא = פנים ואחור face or front and back; forward and backward.

פ״ומ = פרנס ומנהיג a pastor and manager.

פ״ז = פנים זועפות sad looks.

פ״ח = פתרון חלומות the interpretation of dreams; פעל חוזר a reflexive verb.

פ״חד = פרי חדש a new fruit; N.B.

פ״ט = פה טמון here is buried; פרותיו טבין its fruits are good.

---

* See note page 30.

פ"י = פירש he explains; פני יצחק the face of Isaac; N. B.; פא יוד a verb having י for its first radical; פעל יוצא a transitive verb.

פ"כה = פרק כל הצלמים the chapter of the Talmud commencing with the words כל הצלמים

פ"כב = פרק כל כתבי the chapter of the Talmud commencing with the words כל כתבי

פ"כצ = פרק כיצר צולין the chapter of the Talmud commencing with the words כיצר צולין

פ"ל = פרח לבנון the flower of Lebanon; N. B.

פ"מ = פני משה the face of Moses; N. B.

פ"מא = פרח מטה אהרון the rod of Aaron budded; N. B.

פ"מג = פרי מגדים precious fruits; N. B.

פ"מס = פנים מסבירות a smiling face; N. B.

פ"נ = פא נון a defective verb having נ for its first radical; פה נטמן here is buried; פה נקבר here is entombed; פריון נפש the ransom or redemption of a soul.

פ"ס = פתוחה סתומה an open paragraph, a closed paragraph.*

פ"ע = פעל עומד an intransitive verb; פתח ענים an open place.

פע"הק = פה עיר הקודש here in the holy city of–.

* The open paragraph is so called because it commenced the line; and the other closed, because it is separated within the line by a space.

פע"ר = פענח רזא the revealer of secrets; N. B.

פ"פ = פתחון פה an excuse; hope; פאפעל first radical letter.

פ"ציח = פי צדיק יהגה חכמה the mouth of the righteous meditates on wisdom.

פ"ק = פרוטא קטנה a small coin; a farthing; פרק קמה the first chapter; פרוש קונטרים explanatory notes; פורים קטן the little Purim.

פ"ר = פלח רמון a piece of pomegranate; N. B.; פרדם רמונים an orchard of pomegranates.

פ"רא = פרקי רבי אליעזר chapters of Rabbi Eliezer; N. B.

פר"דם = פשט רמז דרש סוד literal sense, figurative sense, explanatory sense, mysterious sense; the four different modes of interpreting the Holy Scripture.

פר"דק = פרוש רבי דוד קמחי commentary of Rabbi David Kimchi.

פ"רח = פירש רבי חננאל Rabbi Channanel explains; פרי חדש a new fruit; N. B.

פ"רמ = פרקי משה chapters of Moses; N. B.

פר"מא = פרח מטה אהרון the rod of Aaron budded; N. B.

פר"שי = פרוש רבי שלמה יצחקי commentary of Rabbi Shelomo Ishaki.

פ"רת = פירש רבינו תם our Rabbi Tam explains.

פ"ש = פרק שירה the chapter containing the song of objects in nature; N. B.; פי שנים double portion; doubly.

פ"ת = פתח תקוה the gate of hope ; N. B.

פ"תח = פנימית תיכון חיצון inner, middle, outter.

פ"תי = פתיחה an opening; the introduction of a book.

פ"תל = פן תמצא לומר perhaps you will find an occasion to say.

אות צ

צ" stands for 90.

צ"א = צד אחד one side; צד אחר another side.

צ"אל = צריך אתה לומר you are required to say.

צ"ב = צאן ברזל sheep considered as iron.

צ"ג = צום גדליה the fast of Gedaliah ; צדיק גמור a perfectly righteous man.

צג"ומ = צעקה גדולה ומרה a great and bitter cry.

צ"ד = צמח דוד the Branch or Sprout of David ; the Messiah ; N. B. ; צוף דבש a honeycomb ; N. B.

צ"ה = צרור המור a bundle of myrrh ; N. B.; צרי היגון sorrowful afflictions ; צאת הכוכבים the rising of stars; צומת הגידים a knot or contraction of the senews.

צה"יוט = צד היותר טוב the better side.

צ"הכ = צאת הכוכבים the rising of stars.

צ"וא = צדקה ואמונה righteousness and truth.

צ"וד = צפון ודרום north and south.

צ"וץ = צדקתך וצדקתך צדקתך the three verses namely Psalm XXXVI. 7; LXXI. 19; and CXIX, 142; which are recited on Sabbath days in the afternoon prayer.

צ"יצית = צדיק יפריד ציציותיו תמיד the righteous separates his fringes always.

צ"ל = צריך להיות it is required to be–; צריך לומר it is required to say ; צידה לדרך provision for the way.

צ"ע = צורך ענין a requisite ; a thing necessary in a matter ; צריך עיון it requires consideration.

צע"גומר = צעקה גדולה ומרה a great and bitter cry.

צ"פח = צפנת פענח חדש the new revealer of secrets; N. B.

צ"פט = צפנת פענח טראני the revealer of secrets by Taranee ; N. B.

צ"ת = צדקת תמים the righteousness of the perfect.

אות ק

ק" stands for 100 ; also for קרי reading ; קשה stiff; difficult ; קמא first ; קמץ the first vowel point.

ק"א = קרבן אהרון the offering of Aaron ; N. B.

ק"ב = קול בכים the voice of mourners ; N. B.

ק"בה = קדוש ברוך הוא or קודשא בריך הוא The Holy One who is Blessed.

ק"ג = קהל גדול or קהלה גדולה a great congregation ; קנין גמור a perfect oath.

ק"גוש = קנין גמור ושלם a perfect and full oath.

ק"ד = קיקיון דיונה Jonah's gourd; N. B.; קורט דם a drop of blood.

ק״די = קדוש ישראל The Holy One of Israel.

ק״הק = קודש הקדשים the holy of holies.

ק״הת = קריאת התורה the reading of the Law.

ק״ו = קל וחומר an inference from minor to major.

ק״וי = קול יעקב the voice of Jacob ; N. B.

קו״יה = קול יהודה the voice of Judah ; N. B.

ק״ח = קנה חכמה acquire wisdom ; he acquired wisdom.

קט״רת = קדושה טהרה רחמים תקוה holiness, purity, mercy, hope.

ק״י = קול יהודה the voice of Judah ; N. B.; קהלת יעקב the congregation of Jacob ; קדיש יתום the praise called קדיש repeated by an orphan.

ק״יל = קיימא לן it is confirmed with us.

ק״ים = קריעת ים סוף the dividing of the Red Sea.

ק״ל = קל להבין easy to understand ; קשה לי it is difficult for me ; קשייא לי he questioned me ; he objected to my proposition.

ק״לה = קודש ליי holy unto God ; dedicated to the worship of God.

ק״מ = קרבן מנחה an offering of a gift ; a meat offering ; N. B.

ק״מל = קא משמע לן it teaches us.

ק״ס = קנין סודר an oath upon an handkerchief

* This is the first of the thirteen logical rules laid down by Rabbi Ishmael for expounding the Law.

or any other article fit to be sworn upon.

ק״סד = קא סלקא דעתך do you suppose ?

ק״עד = קונטרים עגונות דאיתתא notes on the laws of the seclusion of a deserted wife.

ק״ק = קהל קדוש or קהלה קדושה a holy congregation ; קודש קדשים holy of holies.

ק״קק = קדוש קדוש קדוש Holy, Holy, Holy.

קר״הת = קריאת התורה the reading of the Law.

קר״ובץ = קול רנה וישועה באהלי צדיקים the voice of rejoicing and salvation is in the tabernacles of the righteous.

ק״ש = קריאת שמע the recital of שמע ישראל "Hear O Israel the Lord our God is one Lord."

ק״שה = קרא שנא הלכה he read and studied הלכה.

ק״ת = קדיש תתקבל a praise in the liturgy called קדיש containing a sentence commencing with the word תתקבל.

אות ר

ר״ stands for 200 ; also for רב. רבי. רבן Rabbi.

ר״א = רב אלעזר Rabbi Elazar ; רבי אמר the Rabbi says ; רצוף אהבה paved with love ; ראש אשמורות first watch of the night ; רבי אליעזר Rabbi Eliezer.

רא״בד = רבי אברהם בן דוד Rabbi Abraham the son of David ; רבי אברהם בר דיאור Rabbi Abraham the son of Deor.

רא״בח = רבי אליהו בן חיים Rabbi Elijah the son of Haeem.

רא״ביה = רבי אליעזר בן יוסי הגלילי Rabbi Eliezer the son of Yose the Galilean.

רא״בן = רבי אלעזר בן נתן Rabbi Elazar the son of Nathan.

רא״בע = רבי אברהם בן עזרה Rabbi Abraham the son of Ezra generally known as Eben Ezra.

ר״אמ = ראש אמנה the top of Amana*; N. B.; רבי אליה מזרחי Rabbi Elijah Mizrachee.

ר״אש = רבי אהרן ששון Rabbi Aaron Sason.

ר״ב = רפדוני בתפוחים comfort me with apples; N. B.

רב״ים = רומיים בבליים יונים מדים Romans, Babylonians, Grecians, Medians.

רב״שע = רבונו של עולם O Lord of the universe.

ר״ג = רישגמרא the commencement of the Gemara; רבן גמליאל Rabban Gamliel; רבינו גרשום our Rabbi Gershom.

רג״מה = רבינו גרשון מאור הגולה our Rabbi Gershon, the light of the captivity.

ר״ד = רבוני דעלמה O Lord of the universe; ראשית דבר the beginning of a thing; ראשית דעת the beginning of understanding; ראש דוד the head of David; N. B.

רד״בז = רבי דוד בן זמרא Rabbi David the son of Zimra.

---

* Amana is the name of a part of Mount Lebanon.

ר"דכ = רבי דוד כהן Rabbi David the priest.

רד"לא = רישא דלא אתידע the Beginning or Source which is not known.

ר"דק = רבי דוד קמחי Rabbi David Kimchi.

ר"ה = רבון העולמים O Lord of the worlds; רשות הרבים a publice jurisdiction; a public place; ראש השנה the New Year's Day.

ר"הח = ראש החודש the New Moon.

ר"הי = רשות היחיד a private jurisdiction; a private place.

ר"הר = רשות הרבים a public jurisdiction; a public place.

ר"וא = רוממות אל high praises of God.

רו"הק = רוח הקודש the holy spirit.

ר"וח = רוח חן the spirit of grace.

ר"וש = רוב שלום many compliments.

ר"זל = רבותינו זכרונם לברכה our Rabbies of blessed memory.

ר"ח = רחמנא the of Merciful; ראש חודש a New Moon; ראשית חכמה the beginning of wisdom; N. B.; רוח חיים the spirit of life; רב הסדא Rab Hasda; רבינו חננאל our Rabbi Channanel; רבי חנניה Rabbi Channanyah.

ר"חו = רבי חיים ויטאל Rabbi Haeem Weetal.

רה"ויל = רוב חיים ושלום יוסיפו לך may long life and much peace be increased unto you.

ר"חכ = רבי חיים כהן Rabbi Haeem the priest.

רחל = רחמנא לצילן may the Merciful deliver us.

ר"ט = רבינו טוביה our Rabbi Tobia; רבי טרפון Rabbi Tarphon.

ר"י = ראש ישיבה the principal of a college; רבי יוסי Rabbi Yose; רבי יהודה Rabbi Judah; רבי ישמעאל Rabbi Ishmael; רבינו ירוחם our Rabbi Yeruham.

רי"בא = רבי יעקב בן אליעזר Rabbi Jacob the son of Eliezer.

רי"בג = רבי יוסף בן גוריון Rabbi Joseph the son of Gorcon.

ריבה = רבי יעקב בעל הטורים Rabbi Jacob the author of בעל הטורים.

רי"בז = רבי יוחנן בן זכאי Rabbi Jochanan the son of Zakkai.

רי"בל = רבי יהושוע בן לוי Rabbi Joshua the son of Levi; רבי יוסף בן לב Rabbi Joseph the son of Leb.

רי"במ = רבי יוסף בר מאיר Rabbi Joseph the son of Meir.

רי"בן = רבי יצחק בר נתן Rabbi Isaac the son of Nathan.

רי"בר = רבי יעקב בי רב Rabbi Jacob Be Rab.

רי"בש = רבי יצחק בר ששת Rabbi Isaac the son of Sheshath.

ר"יג = רבי יהודה גאון Rabbi Judah Gaon.*

ר"יה = רבי ינאי הכהן Rabbi Yanai the priest.

* The word גאון literally means eminence; but it is also a title added to the name of certain eminent Rabbies.

רי"ו = רבי יעקב ווייל Rabbi Jacob Waweel.

ר"יט = רבי יוסף טראני Rabbi Joseph Tarance.

רי"טבא = רבי יום טוב בר אברהם Rabbi Yom Tob the son of Abraham.

רי"טץ = רבי יום טוב צהלון Rabbi Yom Tob Sahlon.

ר"יל = רבי יצחק לוריא Rabbi Isaac Luria.

ר"ימ = רבי יהודה מינץ Rabbi Judah Mentz.

ר"ינ = רבי יהודה נקדן Rabbi Judah Nakdan.

ר"יק = רבי יוסף קולון Rabbi Joseph Kolon.

ר"ית = רוח יי תניחנו may the spirit of the Lord lead him.

ר"ל = רבי לוי Rabbi Levi; רוצה לומר wishing or meaning to say; רצה לומר he wished or meant to say; ראוי לתקן fit to amend; ריש לקיש Resh Lakish; N. R.; the chief of a band of robbers.

רל"בג = רבי לוי בן גרשום Rabbi Levi the son of Gershom.

ר"מ = רבי מאיר Rabbi Meir; רעיא מהימנא the faithful Shepherd; Moses; ריש מתיבתא the principal of a college; ריש מתא the chief of a city or place.

ר"מא = רבי מאיר אומר Rabbi Meir says; רבי משה איסרלש Rabbi Moses Esralash; רבי משה אלשיך Rabbi Moses Alshech.

רמ"בה = רבי מאיר בעל הנס Rabbi Meir worker of wonders.

רמ"בם = רבי משה בר מימון Rabbi Moses the son

of Maimon, generally known as Maimonides.

רמ"בן = רבי משה בר נחמן Rabbi Moses the son of Nachman, generally known as Nachmanides; רבי מאיר בר נתן Rabbi Meir the son of Nathan.

רמב"עה = רבי מאיר בעל הנס Rabbi Meir worker of wonders.

ר"מג = רבי משה גלאנטי Rabbi Moses Galanti.

ר"מז = רבינו משה זכות our Rabbi Moses Zekhuth.

ר"מח = רבי משה חזן Rabbi Moses Hazzan or Minister; the numerical value of this abbreviation shows also the 248 negative precepts, and the 248 members in the human body.

ר"מך = רבי משה כהן Rabbi Moses the priest.

ר"מל = רבי מאיר לובלין Rabbi Meir Lublin.

ר"ממ = רבי משה מינץ Rabbi Moses Mentz.

ר"מק = רבינו משה קורדווידו our Rabbi Moses Cordaviro.

ר"נ = רעה נאמן the faithful Shepherd; Moses; רבינו נסים our Rabbi Nissim.

ר"נג = רבינו נחשון גאון our Rabbi Nahshon Gaon.

ר"ס = ראש סימן the beginning of chapter—.

ר"סג = רבינו סעדיה גאון our Rabbi Saadiah Gaon.

ר"ע = רבי עקיבה Rabbi Akiba; רבי עזריה Rabbi Azariah.

ר"עא = רבי עקיבה אומר Rabbi Akiba says; רבי

עזריה אומר Rabbi Azariah says; ראש עמוד ראשון the top of the first page or column.

ר״עה = רבינו עליו השלום our Rabbi may peace be on him.

ר״פ = רב פנינים many pearls; N. B.; ראש פסוק the beginning of sentence—; ראש פרק the beginning of chapter—; רבי פלוני Rabbi so and so.

ר״צו = רודף צדקה וחסד he that followeth after righteousness and mercy; רודפי צדקה וחסד they that follow after righteousness and mercy.

ר״קה - רבינו קולונימוס הזקן our Rabbi Colonimos the old.

ר״רש = רוב רובי שלומות many many compliments

ר״ש = רבן שמעון Rabban Simeon; רמת שמואל Samuel's Ramah *; N. B.; רבנו שלמה our Rabbi Solomon; ראש שעיר the head of a goat; ראש שנים the beginning of years.

רש״בא = רבינו שמעון בן אברהם our Rabbi Simeon the son of Abraham; רבי שלמה בן אדרת Rabbi Solomon the son of Addereth.

רש״בג = רבן שמעון בן גמליאל Rabban Simeon the son of Gamliel.

רש״בי = רבי שמעון בר יוחאי Rabbi Simeon the son of Yohai.

---

* Ramah is the name of a city where Samuel the prophet and his parents lived.

רש"בל = רבי שמעון בן לוי Rabbi Simeon the son of Levi; רבי שמעון בן לקיש Rabbi Simeon the son of Lakish.

רש"במ = רבי שמעון בן מאיר Rabbi Simeon the son of Meir.

רש"בץ = רבי שלמה בר צדוק Rabbi Solomon the son of Sadok.

רש"דמ = רבי שלמה די מדינא Rabbi Solomon De Medina.

ר"שט = רב שם טוב Rab Shem Tob.

ר"שי = רבי שלמה יצחקי Rabbi Solomon Ishaki, generally known as Rashi; רבי שלמה ירחי Rabbi Solomon Yarchi; ראש שבטי ישראל the head of the tribes of Israel.

ר"שך = רבי שלמה כהן Rabbi Solomon the priest.

ר"של = רבי שלמה לוריא Rabbi Solomon Luria.

רש"לע = רבונו של עולם Lord of the universe.

ר"שמ = רצונו של מקום the will of the Omnipresent.

ר"ת = רבינו תם Our Rabbi Tam; ראשי תיבות initial letters or abbreviations.

אות ש

ש" stands for 300; at the beginning of words for the relative pronoun אשר who, which or that; and for the conjunction that; also for שער a gate; a part generally of a book.

ש״א = שער אחד a gate; a part; שער ראשון the first gate; the first part; שמואל ראשון First book of Samuel; שבוע ראשונה the first week; שער אפרים the gate of Ephraim; N. B.; שאר אפרים the remnant of Ephraim; N. B.; שערי אורה the gates of light or prosperity שבילי אמונה the ways of faith; N. B.

ש״אא = שאי אפשר which is impossible.

ש״אי = שארית יעקב the remnant of Jacob; N. B.

שא״יל = שומר אמת ישמרהו לעד may He who observes truth protect him for ever.

שא״לכ = שאם לא כן which if not so.

שא״צל = שאין צריך לומר which is not required to be said; שאינה צריכה לגופה which is not required for its purpose.

ש״ב = שאר בשרי near of my kin; שאר בתרי my kin after me; שוכן במקומו one dwelling in his place.

שב״די = שבארבע יסודות which is, or which are in the four elements.

ש״בי = שבט יהודה the tribe of Judah; the sceptre of Judah; N. B.

ש״בנ = שום בר נש any son of man; any human being.

שב״עפ = שבעל פה which is oral.

ש״ג = שלטי גבורים shields of mighty men; N. B.; של גוים belonging to the gentiles.

ש״ד = שער ארבע the fourth gate; the fourth part;

שרש דבר the root of a word; the source of a thing; שפיכות דמים bloodshed; שפטי דעת the lips of understanding; N. B.; שערי דורא the gates of the plain of Dura; N. B.; שפיר דמי a good resemblance.

ש"די = שלמה דוד ישי Solomon, David, Jesse; שומר דירת ישראל the Guardian of the dwelling of Israel.

ש"דר = שליח דרחמנא a messenger of the Merciful, a title given to a messenger from the Holy Land sent to make a collection in aid of some charitable institution.

ש"ה = שער השם the gate of the Lord; שבת היום it is Sabbath to-day; ששנת העמקים the lily of the valleys; N. B.; שיר השירים the Song of songs; N.B.; שלשלת הקבלה a chain of traditions; N. B.; שכן הסכים who decides thus; שאני הכא it differs here; שאני התם it differs there.

שה"זג = שהזמן גרמא which is occasioned or specified by time.

שה"ילל = שהיה לו לומר that he had to say.

שה"יפהי = שבת היום פסח היום it is Sabbath to-day, it is Passover to-day.

ש"המ = שלמה המלך King Solomon; שם המפורש the ineffable name of God.

ש"הס = שהוא סוד which is a mystery; שהם סודות which are mysteries.

ש"הע = שושנת העמקים the lily of the valleys; N. B.; שם העצם a substantive.

שה"עה = שלמה המלך עליו השלום King Solomon may peace be on him.

ש"הש = שיר השירים the Song of songs; N. B.

ש"הת = שם התאר an adjective.

ש"ו = שתי וערב warp and woof; a cross.

ש"וא = שום אחד any one.

ש"וב = שוחט ובודק the slaughterer and examiner (of meat); שחיטה ובריקה slaughtering and examining (meat).

שוב"בים = שמות וארא בא בשלח יתרו משפטים the first six Parashiyoth of the book of Exodus; fasts observed on Mondays and Thursdays of the weeks during which these Parashiyoth are read.

שו"כט = שלום וכל טוב peace and every good.

ש"ות = שאלות ותשובות questions and answers.

ש"ז = שם זכר a masculine noun; שכבת זרע conjugal intercourse; seed of copulation.

ש"ח = שנאת חנם causeless enmity; envy; שנות חיים years of life; N. B.

ש"חק = שוא חולם קמץ Sheva, Cholem, Kamets, three vowel points.

ש"ט = שם טוב a good name; שוחר טוב he that seeketh good.

ש"טח = שטר חוב a bond of debt.

שט"חז = שטר חוב זה this bond of debt.

ש"י = שבות יעקב the Captivity of Jacob; N. B.; שפת ישראל the language of Israel; N. B.; שפתי ישנים

the words of old men; N. B.; שורש ישי the root of Jessi; N. B.; שמו יתברך His blessed name; של יד of the hand; שארית יוסף the remnant of Joseph; N. B.; שם ישר a noun in the nominative case.

שי"בה = שתיקה יפה בשעת התפלה silence is appropriate at the time of prayer.

שי"דח = שתי ידות דרך חכמה double guide to the way of wisdom; N. B.

שי"לא = שלום יהיה לו אמן may peace be unto him; Amen.

שי"ליטא = שיחיה לימים טובים אמן that he may live a happy life; Amen.

שי"לת = שויתי יי לנגדי תמיד I place God always before me.

ש"ינ = שיחיה נצח that he may live for ever.

ש"כ = שפתי כהן the lips of a priest; N. B.

ש"כה = שכן הסכים who decides thus.

ש"כל = שכחה לקט (rules about the sheaf) forgotten in the field at the time of gleaning; שכולו לקט the whole of which is to be gleaned; the whole of which is in extracts.

ש"כמ = שבת כלה מלכתא Sabbath is a bride and a queen.

שכ"מה = שכרך כפול מן השמים may thy reward be double from heaven.

שכנ"הג = שירי כנסת הגדולה the surviving members of the Great Synagogue.

ש"ל = שבולת לקט a gleaned ear of corn; N. B.;

שייך לעיל agreeable to the above; שחטאנו לפניך which we have sinned against thee; שלמה לוריא Solomon Luria.

ש"לה = שני לוחות הברית the two tables of the covenant; N. B.

שלי"טא = שיחיה לימים טובים אמן that he may live a happy life; Amen.

של"ית = שבח לאל יתברך praise or thanks to the blessed God.

ש"לש = שלום לך שלום peace, peace be unto thee.

ש"מ = שמע מניה we understand or learn from it; שכיב מרע lying on deathbed; של מעלה celestial; שלחן מלכים the table of kings; royal feast.

שמ"ות = שנים מקרא ואחד תרגום reading every verse of the text of the Law twice and its Chaldee paraphrase once.

ש"מע = שחרית מנחה ערבית the morning, the afternoon, and the evening prayer.

ש"מש = שם משותף a name applicable to different things.

ש"נ = שנאמר as it is said; שם נקבה a feminine noun; שם נוטה a collective noun.

ש"נב = שהכל נהיה בדברו by Whose word or command all things came into existence.

ש"נח = שוא נח a silent Sheva.

ש"נב = שחיטת נכרי נבלה meat slaughtered by a gentile is like a carcass.

ש"נע = שוא נע a vocal Sheva.

ש"נפ = שלא נזכר פעלו one whose work is not remembered or considered.

ש"ס = ששה סדרים the six orders or parts of the Mishna.

ש"סה = the numerical value of this abbreviation shows the 365 affirmative precepts corresponding to the 365 veins in the human frame and to the number of days in a year.

ש"ע = שמיני עצרת the eighth day of the Feast of Tabernacles; שלחן ערוך a prepared table; N. B.; שמנה עשרה eighteen blessings.*

ש"עד = שערי דמעה the gates of tears ; N. B.

שע"טנז = שוע טווי נוז carding,spinning, twisting.

ש"עכ = שם עצם כללי a common noun.

שע"כזי = שלום על כל זרע ישראל peace to the whole seed of Israel.

ש"עפ = שם עצם פרטי a proper noun.

שע"ריל = שלחן ערוך רבי יצחק לוריא the book called שלחן ערוך by Rabbi Isaac Luria.

ש"עש = שערי שמשון the gates of Samson ; N. B.

ש"פ = שוה פרוטה worth a farthing.

ש"פא = שפתי אמת the lips of truth ; N. B.

ש"פט = שפע טל the abundance of dew ; N. B.

ש"פי = שומר פתאים יי the Lord is the protector of the simple.

---

* See note page 51.

ש״פר = שפתי רננות the singing lips; N. B.

ש״צ = שערי צדק the gates of righteousness; N. B.; שליח צבור the messenger i. e. the minister of a congregation.

שצמ״חנכל = שבתאי Saturn; צדק Jupiter; מאדים Mars; חמה the Sun; נוגה Venus; כוכב Mercury; לבנה the Moon.

ש״ק = שבת קודש the holy Sabbath.

ש״ר = שלום רב much peace; many compliments; שבע רצון satisfied with favour; N. B.; שמות רבא the allegorical exposition of the book of Exodus.

ש״רי = שם רשעים ירקב the name of the wicked shall rot.

שרל״תולמ = שלום רב לאוהבי תורתך ואין למו מכשול great peace have they who love thy Law, they shall have no stumbling block.

ש״ש = שבועת שוא a vain or unnecessary oath; שבועת שקר a false oath; שם שמים the name of God; שים שלום keep peace; the last portion of the עמידה or the prayer offered silently; שני שרשים two roots; שמע שלמה the fame of Solomon; N. B.

ש״של = שם שמים לבטלה the name of God in vain.

ש״ת = שלמא תנינא a second compliment; שמא תימא perhaps you will say; שמחת תורה the rejoicing of the Law; the ninth or last day of the Feast of Tabernacles; שבת תשובה the Sabbath of repentance i.e.

the Sabbath that falls within the ten penitential days; שומע תפלה the Hearer of Prayer; God.

ת

ת״ stands for 400; at the beginning of words as the sign of the second person and third person feminine; and at the end of the second person; also for תשובת the answer of—; תקון ordination or direction; תחת instead of; under; תמורת a substitute of–.

ת״א = תרגום אחר another paraphrase or interpretation; תרגום אונקלוס the Chaldee paraphrase by Onkelos; תנחומות אל divine consolations; N. B.; תענית אסתר the Fast of Esther; תולדות אהרון the generations of Aaron; notes of reference in some editions of the Scripture showing where certain passages are quoted in the Talmud.

ת״או = תולדות אדם וחוה the generations of Adam and Eve; N. B.; תורת אדם וחוה the law of Adam and Eve.

תא״מכ = תורה אור מנחת כהן the Law is light, the gift of a priest; N. B.

ת״ב = תשעה באב the ninth day of the month of Ab or the Day of Lamentation; תנא בתרא the latter Rabbi.

תב״חט = תִכתב בספר חיים טובים may thou be enlisted in the book of happy life.

תבכ״כבנ = תפלה בלא כוונה כגוף בלא נשמה a prayer without devotion is like a body without soul.

ת״ג = תנועה גדולה a long vowel; תרועה גדולה a

great sound of alarm; תלישא גדולה the tonic accent called great Telisha.

ת"ד = תמים דעים persons perfect in knowledge; תשלום דגש the compensation of Dagseh.

ת"ה = תחית המתים the resurrection of the dead; תפלת הדרך the prayer of a traveller before setting out on a journey; תורת הבית the law of the house; N.B.; תרומת הדשן a gift of a fat thing; תפארת הגרשוני the glory of the Gershonite; N. B.; תורת העולה the law of the burnt offering; N. B.; תורת האשם the law of the trespass offering; N. B.

תה"ל = תהלה לדוד David's psalm of praise; N. B.

תה"למ = תהלה למשה Moses' psalm of praise; N. B.

ת"הפ = תואר הפעל an adverb.

ת"ו = תבנה ותכונן may it be built and established.

תו"א = תורה אור the Law is light; notes of reference in the Talmud showing where Scripture passages are quoted from; N. B.

תו"בב = תבנה ותכונן במהרה בימינו may it be built and established soon in our days.*

ת"וד = תומר דבורה the palm tree of Debora; N. B.

תו"הק = תורתנו הקדושה our holy Law.

ת"וח = תורת חיים the law of life.

* A phrase used after the names of the cities in the Holy Land, especially Jerusalem, Hebron, Tiberias and Safed.

תו״י = תולדות יצחק the generations of Isaac; N. B.; תולעת יעקב thou worm, O Jacob !* N. B.

תו״יש = תומת ישרים the innocence of the upright; N. B.

ת״ומ = תורת משה the Law of Moses.

תוש״לבע = תם ונשלם שבח לאל בורא עולם complete and perfect is the praise of God, Creator of the world; it is finished and completed, praise be to God, the Creator of the world; Finis.†

ת״ז = תקון זהר the direction or ordination of the Zohar; N. B.; תקוני זהר the directions or ordinations of the Zohar; N. B.

ת״ח = תורת חיים the law of life; תלמיד חכם a learned man; תלמידי חכמים learned men; תורת חכם the law of a wise man; תא חזי come and see; תענית חלום a fast held on account of a bad dream; תורת חטאת the law of the sin offering.

ת״חס = תורת חסד the law of mercy.

ת״י = תקונים directions or ordinations; תרגום יונתן the Targum or Chaldee paraphrase by Jonathan; תרגום ירושלמי the Targum or Chaldee paraphrase called the Jerusalem Targum; תפארת ישראל the beauty or glory of Israel; N. B.; תולדות יצחק the generations of Isaac; N. B.; תולעת יעקב thou worm, O Jacob! N. B.; תענית יחיד the fast of a single person; תומת ישרים the innocence of the upright; תחת יד in the possession of–.;

---

* This phrase is used in Isaiah XII. 14 for the congregation of Israel.

† This phrase is used at the end of a book.

under the authority of—.

ת״יט = תוספות יום טוב Super-commentary on the tract of the Talmud on holidays called יום טוב.

תי״קו = תשבי יתרץ קושיות ובעיות (Elijah) the Tishbite will solve the difficulties and questions.

ת״כ = תורת כהנים the Levitical Law; תניא כותיה the הלכה or rule is according to him or it; תקפו כהן the might of a priest; N. B.

ת״ל = תהלות לאל praised be God; תלמוד לומר the Talmud says; תרצה לידע you wish to know; תרי לשני two meanings; תאוה לענים pleasant to the eyes.

ת״לח = תהלות לאל חי praised be the living God.

תל״ית = תהלות לאל יתברך praised be God who is blessed.

ת״מ = תברך מנשים blessed be she above women, a complimentary phrase used after the name of a woman.

ת״מכ = תהי מנוחתו כבוד may his rest be glorious.*

תמכ״עוכי = תהי מיתתו כפרה עליו ועל כל ישראל may his death be an atonement for him and for all the Israelites.*

ת״נ = תולדות נח tha generations of Noah; N. B.

תנ״בעא = תהי נפשו בגן עדן אמן may his soul be in the Garden of Eden; Amen.*

ת״נה = תניא נמי הכי the Beritha or the supplement to the Mishna also says thus.

---

* This is a phrase used after the name of a deceased person.

תנה"ים = תפארת נצח הוד יסוד מלכות beauty, triumph; glory, basis, kingdom, the divine attributes.

תנ"ך = תורה נביאים כתובים the Law, the Prophets, the Hagiographa.

תנצב"ה = תהי נפשו צרורה בצרור החיים may his soul be bound up in the band of the living.*

ת"ס = תקון סופרים emendations of the scribes; N. B.

ת"ע = תרי עשר the twelve minor prophets; תפלת ערבית the evening prayer.

ת"עב = תבוא עליו ברכה may blessing come upon him.

ת"עח = תעלומות חכמה the mysteries of wisdom; N. B.

ת"פי = תפארת ישראל the glory of Israel.

תפ"יג = תפארת ישראל גדול the greater book called תפארת ישראל.

תפ"יק = תפארת ישראל קטן the smaller book called תפארת ישראל.

ת"פל = תפלה למשה the prayer of Moses; N. B.

ת"פש = תפארת שמואל the glory of Samuel; N.B.

תפ"שת or **תש"ת** = תפלת שכור תועבה the prayer of an intoxicated person is an abomination.

ת"צ = תענית צבור the fast of a congregation.

ת"ק = תנועה קטנה a short vowel; תנא קמא the former Rabbi; תורה קטן the Law in miniature.

* See note page 119.

ת״ר = תרגום the Chaldee paraphrase of the Scripture; תנו רבנן the Rabbies teach ; תחום רבא a great abyss.

ת״רי = תלמידי רבינו יונה the scholars of our Rabbi Jonah.

ת״ש = תא שמע come and hear; תוספות שבת a supercommentary on the laws of the Sabbath.

ת״שי = תפילין של יד the phylacteries for the hand.

ש״בכ = תורה שבכתב the written Law.

תש״בעפ = תורה שבעל פה the oral Law.

תש״בר = תינוקות של בית רבן infants attending school.

ת״שר = תפילין של ראש the phylacteries for the head.

תש״רת ת״שת ת״רת = in these abbreviations ת = תקיעה ; ש = שברים ; ר = תרועה ; the different modes of blowing the trumpet.

ת״ת = תלמוד תורה the study of the Law.

APPENDIX.

The abbreviations marked with asterisks are repeated in the Appendix for further explanation.

א״ז* = אם זה if this.

א״יה* = אם יגזור השם if God decree.

א״נ* = אי נמי if so.

א״של = אכילה שתיה לְויה eating, drinking and accompanying.

ב״גר* = בגין דהא on this account.

בח״רג = בחרם רבינו גרשום by the excommunication of our Rabbi Gershom.

ב״כר = בר כבוד רבי or בן the son of the honoured gentleman—.

ב״לר = בלשון רומי in Latin.

ב״מא* = בר מן אחד except one.

במ״להק = במלאכת הקודש in a pious work.

ב״ס* = בן סורר a stubborn son; בא סימן we get a sign; here is a sign.

ב״סא = בספרים אחרים in other books.

ב״תכ = בתלמוד כתיב in the Talmud it is written; בתלמוד כן in the Talmud it is so.

ג״נ = גלגולי נשמות the transmigration of souls

ג״אי = גלילות ארץ ישראל the provinces of the Land of Israel.

ד״ה = דברי המחבר the words of the author.

ד״ח* = דברי חכמים the words of wise men.

ד״כ = דרך כלל a general rule.

ה״ב* = הבחור the bachelor—.

ה״בת = הבתולה the virgin—.

ה״ד* = הוא דרך that is the way; הכי דרשינן thus we explain it.

ה״דא* = הכל דבור אחד all that is one saying.

*ה"ה = החכם הגדול the very learned man ;

ה"זמ = הרי זה משבח behold this is praiseworthy.

הח"הש = החכם השלם the perfectly wise man.

ה"נה = הנשר הגדול the Great Eagle, a name given to Maimonides by way of eminence.

*ה"ק = הכי קתני thus he says or teaches.

וב"כא = ובכל אחד and in each.

*ז"אז = זה אחר זה one after another.

ז"גכ = זה גם כן also this.

ז"הד = זה הדבר this thing.

*ח"ב = חתן בראשית the Bridegroom of the Beginning i. e. one appointed to recommence the reading of the Law on the last day of the Feast of Tabernacles.

ח"ע = חזון עובדיה the vision of Obadiah ; N. B.

ח"ת = חתן תורה the Bridegroom of the Law i. e. one appointed to read the last section of the Law on the last day of the Feast of Tabernacles.

י"הע = יגן יי עליכם may God protect you.

*כ"וכ = כמה וכמה how much more.

כמ"שד = כמו שדרשו as they expounded.

*ל"ד = לדעתי to my knowledge.

*ל"י = לשנא יתירה additional saying.

*ל"מ = לשון משנה the language of the Mishna.

למ"נמ = למא נפקא מנה what do we infer from it.

ל"פל = לית פליג ליה there is no controversy about it.

מ"דח = מתחיל דבור חדש one who or that which begins a new thing or subject.

מ"הד = מהו דתימא what is it that you say.

מל"הק = מלאכת הקודש a pious work.

מ"שכ = מה שכתוב כאן what is written here.

ס"ג* = סוד גדול a great mystery.

ס"המ* = סם המות poison.

ס"י* = ספר ישן an old book.

ע"* = ערך the price.

ע"דה* = על דרך המדרש according to the Midrash.

ע"מ* = עול משקץ the perversion of the abominable or idolator.

ע"נל = ענין נזכר למעלה the abovementioned subject.

ע"צ* = עובדי צלמים the worshippers of images.

ע"ש* = עוד שם again there.

פ"ג* = פלוגתה גדולה a great controversy.

ק"אל = קאמר ליה he says to him.

ק"קס = קבול קנין סודר acceptance of the oath on an handkerchief.

ק"שה* = קרה שנא הלכה the Scripture, the Mishna, the Gemara.

ר"בר = רחמנים בני רחמנים the merciful, who are the children of the merciful.

ש"ח* = שומר חנם one who undertakes a charge without any remuneration.

שע"הזל = שחור על הלבן זכר לחרבן white on black is in memory of the destruction of Jerusalem.

ש"ר = שם רע an evil name.

ש"ש* = שומר שכר one who undertakes a charge for wages.

תיוב"תא = תשבי יבא ויגיד בפיו תירוץ אמתי (Elijah) the Tishbite shall come and tell the true explanation with his own mouth.

תם ונשלם ספר ראשי תיבות

זבת תודה לרוכב ערבות:

ERRATA.

Page.	Line.	
4	8	for אוע *read* אוינ
5	9	for לברכח *read* לברכה
8	1	for נמי *read* ניכוא
8	16	for end a sentence *read* end of a sentence.
8	24	for the abbreviation אעג should be above אענע
9	19	for תמורתו אחד *read* אחד חמורתו
10	17	for communtation *read* commutation.
12	8	for רא *read* די
17	16	for word *read* words.
24	8	for the way o *read* the way of.
29	14	for it is he who said *read* this is what they say.
32	13	for הנעלי רבי let my Rabbi enter *read* הנעלה רבי the eminent Rabbi.
37	10	for והלב *read* וחלב
53	21	for ישמועלים *read* ישמועאלים
56	17	for רמי *read* דמי
57	9	for הדב *read* הרב
58	14	for בבוד *read* כבוד
63	21	for o every one *read* to every one,
64	25	for טהול *read* טחול
71	26	for slaughtre *read* slaughter.
67	10	for לברכת *read* לברכה
72	23	for חכמנו *read* הכמינו
73	18	for Gods *read* gods
83	9	for נתנינת *read* נתינת
92	6	for פרוטא *read* פרוטה
103	24	for רהויל *read* רחויל
103	26	for רהכ *read* רחכ

www.ingramcontent.com/pod-product-compliance
Lightning Source LLC
Chambersburg PA
CBHW032007010726
47493CB00007B/2303